THE MCGOWAN TEA PARTY

A LUXE MYSTERY

DEE ERNST

To find more of Dee's books, go to
www.deeernst.com

Comments? Questions? An uncontrollable desire to just chat? You can
reach me at
Dee@deeernst.com

ISBN:9780998033426

❀ Created with Vellum

ALSO BY DEE ERNST

1

"A tea party?" Enza asked, somewhat incredulously. "You want us to do a *tea* party?" She narrowed her eyes and drummed her perfectly manicured nails against the desktop. "Really?"

It's not that Luxe Affairs didn't know how to do a tea party. After all, that's how Vincenza Biondi had started her business, more than five years ago: doing children's birthday parties. Her tea parties for little girls—complete with tiny china cups and saucers and jelly finger sandwiches— had been something Luxe became known for. But she had vowed that, as soon as she was financially able, she would never do another party for anyone under the age of twelve again. A recent sweet-sixteen party had nudged her new line in the sand up to the age of twenty-one. It had been two years and seven months since her last children's birthday party, and she was not about to go back now, tea or no tea.

Enza was approaching fifty, but she never let on how close to landing she was. Her natural love of food and her almost equal love of clothes drove her to the gym four days a week, resulting in a body of equal muscle and curve. Her hair was dark and thick, cut in soft waves to her shoulders, and her eyes were big, black and quite beautiful. She had been turning heads for years, and still worked at it.

She'd been divorced for eight years, but after a few years alone she decided she wanted something to do with her life besides sell commercial real estate in Brooklyn, New York. She sold her condo and moved west, into the wilds of New Jersey, and bought a small row house in Morristown. She turned the first floor into offices for Luxe Affairs, lived on the two upper floors, and advertised as a party planner.

Joanne Collins, who owned one-third of Luxe, nodded solemnly. "Yes. It's actually a very special birthday party."

"Ah, special. Well, then, that makes it all right," Enza said sarcastically. "For who? Kate and William's kids?"

Jo shook her head. "No, and that's the thing." She grinned. "It's for a seventy-year-old lady."

Enza sighed in relief. "Thank you, Jo, for giving me a friggin' heart attack. You could have said that up front."

Jo rolled her eyes. "I know how you feel about kid's parties. Did you honestly think I'd suggest we'd do another?" Jo had been with Enza from the beginning of Luxe. After college she'd spent seven years as the assistant to an in-house events planner for a large insurance company, and when she joined Luxe she was grateful to escape team-building breakfasts and executive retreats. She had suffered with Enza through dealing with spoiled, demanding, and irrational children and their equally spoiled, demanding and irrational parents.

"Where are we doing this?" Enza asked. "Do we need a venue?"

"No," Jo said. Jo usually wasn't the first point of contact with a client. That was Enza's job. Jo dealt with the more practical aspects of the planning: putting together all of

Enza's ideas and figuring out how to make them work. But Enza had been out when the call had come in from Richard McGowan.

Jo had scribbled all the information in a battered Moleskine notebook. She flipped a few pages. "The clients, Richard McGowan and his wife, are throwing this for his mother at their home in Upper Montclair. They have a guest list of about thirty and want a traditional high tea."

Phyllis Anders, the third partner, closed her eyes and sighed with delight. "High tea. I'll do six different finger sandwiches, and scones, of course. Clotted cream," she murmured, half to herself, "and imported Irish butter." She was tall and thin, with boney shoulders and light hair streaked with gray.

Enza raised an eyebrow. "Been thinking about this for a while, Phyl?"

Phyllis smiled wistfully. "I've always wanted a high tea," she said, with the same reverence some people used in asking for a winning lottery ticket, or true love.

Enza nodded. "Okay. Give me a sample menu and costs. Jo, you give a quote?"

Jo shook her head. "I thought you should check out the house and size things up first. Who knows what we'll need."

"Right. Okay, since you first talked to the client, call her—"

"Him. The son."

Okay." She glanced over at Jo. "That's a first for us, no? Have we ever had a man call for a mother's birthday?"

Phyl sighed. "I think it's sweet. He must be very devoted."

"Yeah," Enza snorted. "Or the wife can't be bothered. Call him and make an appointment for me to go over. When are we lookin' here?"

"We have four weeks," Jo said. "The twenty-third. Early Sunday afternoon."

"High tea is usually between five and seven," Phyl said.

"Not if the client wants it in the early afternoon," Enza said, grinning.

"I have a feeling that the client will not be attending," Jo said. "He kept talking about how his mother had worked in a fancy tea shop when she was a girl, and he wanted her to be reminded of that. He made it clear that this was for his mother and all her friends. He said he'd be there, of course, but in another part of the house. He sounded like the type to spend the day sipping vodka martinis."

Enza glanced out the window. The sun was streaming through, a light breeze coming through the screens. What she wouldn't give to be outside, sipping vodka martinis. "Anything else?"

"That's it," Jo said. "Thirty little old ladies eating finger sandwiches and sipping oolong tea. How hard can that be? This one will be a snap."

"You think?" Enza asked. She'd been doing this long enough to know that nothing was ever as easy as it looked. "It better be, cause that wedding coming up in September is heating up and the bride is starting to make noises like a spoiled four-year-old."

Weddings meant big money for Luxe, and Enza worked hard when pitching to brides-to-be the idea that only Luxe could pull off the Wedding of the Century. And Enza and her team always delivered. But all three were getting tired of bridezillas, and lately it seemed that all brides fell into that category.

"Is this the Basking Ridge princess?" Jo asked.

Enza nodded. "Yes. And I'm seeing her again tomorrow.

This one wants an in-person audience to talk about candles."

"We could always stop doing weddings," Phyl suggested. "I mean, are they even worth all the aggravation?"

Enza sighed. "The second van needs a new transmission, we still owe the IRS from last quarter, and Jo here keeps insisting that we pay the staff. So, yeah. We keep doing weddings."

Jo grinned. "Aren't you happy that I found something that's big bucks and no trouble?"

Enza sighed again. "We'll see."

USUALLY, Enza called on their clients alone, but Phyl asked to come along to check out the kitchen to determine how much work could be done on-site, and Enza had to agree it was a valid reason. Both she and Jo avoided driving anywhere with Phyllis because Phyl insisted on doing the driving herself.

Phyllis Anders had gone from being a personal secretary in a major corporation to a Culinary Institute graduate, a sous chef at a ski resort in Colorado, and then on to owning a restaurant in San Francisco for almost a decade. Then eight years ago, she got divorced, lost both her parents and had a disastrous fire in her restaurant, all in a three month period. She spent the next few years wandering from one restaurant to another before heading out to Hoboken, New Jersey, for her cousin's second wedding. Her cousin had hired Luxe for the event, and there Phyl met Enza and Jo.

A conversation was struck up, along with a deal. Luxe was spending too much money on food and was looking for a way to cut out the various caterers they used. Phyl had an impressive culinary resume and enough money to outfit an entire commercial kitchen in the basement of the Luxe row house. So she became the third partner and everyone was very happy with the situation, except when Phyl felt the need to drive.

Phyl had not had a driver's license since her days in Colorado. She hadn't needed one. She walked everywhere she needed to go in San Francisco, or took a cable car. She'd lived in major cities since then and hadn't needed to drive anywhere. Her new license was a badge of honor, and although she had obviously passed the driving test, in the real world she was a terrible driver. Too slow, too cautious, with a tendency to ride the brakes. Enza and Jo kept thinking that Phyl would improve with practice, but so far that had not proved true.

"Phyl, you might want to speed up a bit," Enza suggested.

"The speed limit is twenty-five."

"I know that, but you're going fifteen. Going too slow is just as bad as going too fast."

Getting to Upper Montclair from Morristown involved highway driving as well as bumper-to-bumper in-town traffic, winding side roads, and lots of stop signs. It tended to be a tedious drive, especially during the early morning rush hour. Driving with Phyl turned the trip into a journey of epic proportions.

Phyl tightened her grip on the steering wheel and gently pressed the accelerator a little harder.

Enza had found that being the navigator gave her a perfect excuse to keep focused on her phone, rather than anything that might be happening on the road. Whatever was going to happen, she reasoned, was all about *when*, rather than *if*, and she'd be better off not seeing it coming.

"Take the next left," she said.

Phyl put on her blinker and, naturally, slowed down even more.

"By next left, I mean the road that's beyond this curve, Phyl, not this driveway."

"You know, you're making me very nervous."

Enza took a deep breath and closed her eyes until she felt the car turn, with the speed of an arthritic turtle, onto the side road.

"Good. Now, the fourth house on the right."

They crawled to a stop. Phyl parked the car and breathed a sigh of relief. Enza took another deep breath.

"Phyl, why don't you pull into the driveway?"

"Because I'd have to back out. I hate backing out. I'm always afraid someone will hit me."

"Phyl, this is a residential side street, and it's pretty deserted. I doubt that will be a problem."

"Yes, well, you never know." Phyl turned off the ignition.

"But you can't just leave the car here. You're kind of in the middle of the road. To get around you, people will have to pull into the other lane."

Phyl looked around. "You just said no one would be driving by."

"I said *probably*. At least pull over to the curb."

"You know I hate to park."

"You don't have to park, just pull over so you're not in the middle of the road."

"That's parking."

"Do you want me to do it?"

"No." Phyl started the car and, after seven or eight minutes of going back and forth, was about six inches closer to the curb.

"Perfect," Enza said brightly.

Phyl released her death grip on the steering wheel and turned the ignition off again. "Are you sure? I don't think—"

Enza was already out of the car and walking deliberately up the brick walkway. Phyl hurried after her.

"Did I lock the car?" Phyl wondered.

"Doesn't matter," Enza said shortly, glancing back at Phyl's prized vehicle, and 2012 Subaru Outback, gray, with a crumpled bumper. "In this neighborhood, if someone was going to steal a car, yours would be their last choice." She smoothed her hair and pressed the bell.

Faith McGowan answered the door. "Come in," she said after brief introductions had been made. "Thank you for coming out here so early. I have a series of appointments later today, but I wanted to meet you both and, of course, get this party rolling as soon as possible." She led the two women through a small but gracious foyer into a beautifully decorated main room, where Molly McGowan waited, sitting stiffly in a Queen Anne armchair, with a black cane at her side.

Molly had not had an easy life and was not one of those women who had aged gracefully. She looked every single one of her seventy years. In fact, she looked even older. Her hair was dull gray, put up in an untidy bun. Her skin was sagging and without make-up, giving her a flat, dull look. Her eyes, though, were bright and glittering.

"Mother," Faith said, "This is Enza, who will be organizing your party. And Phyllis, who will be in charge of the food."

Enza crouched a bit and held out her hand. "Pleased to meet you, Mrs. McGowan."

Molly glared at Enza, then the outstretched hand. "You Eyetalian?"

Enza straightened and dropped her hand. She smiled brightly. "Yes. Second generation."

Molly made a noise between a grunt and a wheeze. She turned her eyes to Phyl. "You don't look Eyetalian."

Phyl shook her head. "My maiden name is Felstrum. Swedish."

Molly shrugged. "Whatever. You two are goin' to put together me birthday party?" She had lived in the U.S. for over fifty years but had never lost her thick brogue.

Enza sat opposite Molly and nodded. "Yes." She pulled her bright pink notebook out of her bag. "A high tea? What a wonderful idea."

"It was me son's idea," Molly said. "Why his wife can't manage to put together a party is just beyond me, but it's his money. He can throw it away as he likes."

Faith, standing by the fireplace, cleared her throat. "It's *our* money," she said.

Molly sniffed and made a face.

Enza clicked her pen. "Yes. Well. About thirty people? We'll need a guest list, of course, by the end of the week. We'll send out invitations, probably just a simple embossed card with the date and time. The important thing, of course, is the menu."

Phyl, sitting next to Enza, leaned forward. "A traditional oolong tea, I think."

Molly shook her head. "No caffeine. I can't do caffeine."

"No problem," Phyl said. "We can get decaf. And maybe an herbal as well? Chamomile or maybe citrus?"

"I hate that stupid hippie tea," Molly said.

Phyl's mouth dropped open and she glanced at Enza. "Ah, fine. No herbal tea. Just decaf. Lemon, sugar and milk—"

"No sugar. I got the diabetes. And no milk. Lactose intolerant. So be half o' the guest list," Molly looked smug. "What I do love is some good hot cocoa."

"We can do that with Stevia and almond milk," Phyl countered.

Molly's eyes narrowed.

"Finger sandwiches," Phyl went on bravely. "I bake my own bread, and we can have a white sandwich and a nice egg bread."

"Has to be gluten-free," Molly said, with a smirk.

"We can do that too," Phyl said. "Egg salad, chicken salad, cucumber, plum tomato, and a nice cress, honey ham and Dijon, and probably a shrimp paste."

"Cucumbers repeat on me somethin' awful. Most of me friends as well. Old people can't eat those kinds foods, ya silly twit. And besides, the seeds get stuck in me dentures. So make sure those tomatoes haven't got any seeds, either, hear me? Don't like dark meat chicken neither. And no celery or any other crap in with the chicken. Grapes and such in chicken salad? Bullshit."

"Right," Phyl said. Enza was writing it all down, her jaw tightly clenched.

"No shellfish. Allergic," Molly said.

"Of course," Enza muttered under her breath.

Phyl kicked Enza in the ankle, her smile never cracking even as her high tea dreams sank rapidly. "And of course, scones. Gluten-free scones. No clotted cream, I suppose, but I'll have butter and sugar-free homemade jam."

Molly sat back and nodded slowly. "That sounds fine, I guess. But I do like a sweet. Loved fairy cakes as a young thing."

"But..." Phyl frowned. "Diabetes?"

"Can't you bake with that Stevia crap?" Molly asked, her

mouth smiling as her eyes glittered angrily. "Richard made it sound like your little company knew what it was doing."

Phyl placed her hand on Enza's knee and applied gentle pressure. "Of course we know what we're going, and of course we can make sure your sweet tooth is satisfied," she said "Anything else?"

Molly sat straight up, grabbed the cane, and held out a hand. Enza looked around. Faith was still standing by the fireplace, her arms folded across her chest, her mouth in a thin line.

"I need to get up," Molly snapped.

"You need to ask," Faith shot back.

Enza and Phyl looked at each other. Phyl closed her eyes and breathed out slowly.

"Help me, up," Molly growled. "Please?"

Faith crossed the room, took Molly's hand, and pulled her upright. Without even glancing at her daughter-in-law, Molly jerked her head at Enza and Phyl, who silently got up and followed.

The dining room was high ceilinged and elegant, tall windows overlooking a pool and green sweep of lawn. Molly hobbled to the windows, her cane hitting the floor as she walked, making a steady, loud and annoying thump. She jerked open the sheer drape and nodded to the outside patio. "I want tables set up out there."

Enza jotted in her notebook. "One long table or small, scattered round ones?"

"Scattered, I think. On the lawn, mind you, not the patio. The concrete gets too hot."

Behind her, Enza could hear Faith exhale loudly.

"And umbrellas, o' course," Molly went on. "And there, by the big tree? Put the music there."

Enza glanced at Faith, who raised her eyebrows in surprise.

"Music?" Enza asked. "What kind of music do you like?"

"Irish. What a stupid question. A couple of fiddles and a pipe. And a mandolin. Can't be real Irish music without a mandolin."

"No problem," Enza said. "We can do that."

"I like flowers. Lilies. And real china, now." Molly opened the French door and took a deep breath of the fresh air. "None of that disposable shite. *And* real silver. Linen tablecloths and napkins. Forget candles. Why everyone thinks a table needs a candle in broad daylight is beyond me."

"Agreed," Enza said as she scribbled, gold pen flashing.

"Although you may need to string some lights, in case the party runs a bit long," Molly said.

"Mother," Faith said, her voice pleasant and even. "We talked about this. Your party is going to start in the early afternoon."

"Can't do high tea in the afternoon, girl, I told *you* that." Molly moved her shoulders. "Tea starts at six."

"The party starts at three," Faith said clearly.

"The party can start whenever you like. But tea will be served at six." Molly pushed past Enza and Phyl, back toward the living room. Her footsteps, and the thumping of her cane, faded into silence. Faith closed her eyes, let out a long, heartfelt sigh, and bowed her head.

"Mrs. McGowan?" Enza said gently. "Maybe you could show us the kitchen?"

Faith nodded as she drew herself up. "Of course. This way."

Phyl did not throw herself on her knees and bow down when she saw the kitchen, but the expression on her face gave her away. Double ovens, a six-burner gas stove, and miles of counter space. She placed both hands on the cool granite. "I can do all the cooking right here if you'll let me. That way we don't have to transport so much prepared food." She looked around. There was another set of French doors leading out to the pool. "And we can serve directly from here."

Faith nodded, somewhat listlessly.

"I'll have two of my staff with me, will that be okay?" Phyl asked.

Faith nodded again. "Whatever you need to do to make this the best birthday, tea, whatever party you can make."

Enza looked at Faith curiously. "I know this may be presumptuous of me, but can I tell you? You're being awful accommodating to her. If she were *my* mother-in-law, I'd have locked her in the attic by now."

Faith suddenly smiled, and her whole face changed, becoming almost beautiful. "It's her farewell party. She doesn't know it, but this little extravaganza will be the very last time she eats a gluten-free crumb of anything in this house." She closed her eyes and sighed. "She's been living with us for six months, and she has redefined the idea of for better or worse. She's always hated me. I don't know why, but the situation is impossible. I gave Richard an ultimatum. Maybe that was wrong of me, but...Richard has made his choice, and, thank God, it's one I can live with."

Enza choked back a laugh. "All righty, then. Phyl, you got everything you need?"

Phyl nodded happily, and the two of them followed Faith back to the front door.

Once back in the car, Enza leaned her head back and took a deep breath in preparation for the return trip. Enza, in her little black Mercedes, had been known to make the

Morristown-Montclair run in as little as sixteen minutes, with traffic, and without actually hitting anyone.

"I must say," Phyl said, starting the car, "Molly seems to be a very demanding woman."

"She's a first-class tartar, that's what she is. Faith must have the patience of a friggin' saint." Enza fastened her seat belt. "And remind me to smack Jo upside the head." She pitched her voice higher. "Big bucks and no trouble." Enza snorted. "No trouble my Aunt Fanny. This whole thing is going to be a giant pain in my ass."

Phyl checked her side-view mirror, rearview mirror, looked over her shoulder, and pulled away from the curb. "It's not Jo's fault," she murmured.

"Yeah, whatever. But she's still gonna be the one to pick the seeds out of the friggin' tomatoes." Enza looked at her phone. "So, you're gonna take this right."

"Here?"

"No, Phyl. That's a dead end. See that street sign? *There*."

It was a journey of equally epic proportions back to Morristown.

THE OFFICES of Luxe Affairs were on a quiet Morristown side street in a narrow brick house. There was a neat, cobblestone courtyard with a few tasteful urns planted with equally tasteful annuals. There was even a small wrought iron bench, upon which no client had ever sat. The front door was actually a set of two narrow, wooden doors, painted the same blue as the sign in the front window, which read "Luxe Affairs".

Enza came through the front doors after spending two hours and forty-seven minutes with Vienna Rose LaCosta, a twenty-four-year-old bride who was the only daughter in a family with six boys, as well as being the youngest, and therefore the most spoiled of the children. In other words, a bride from hell.

This was after spending the morning with Molly McGowan. She felt as though God was punishing her for something very particular that she had done, possibly in her other life, if her other life had been spent as a judge during the Salem witch trials.

"She wants a horse-drawn carriage," Enza muttered, walking into the front room and letting her tote bag, shoulder bag, and pink leather notebook all slide to the floor. "Swear to God, a Cinderella carriage. With palominos. Six of them. I didn't know what a friggin' palomino even was. I had to run into the bathroom and Google it. It's a kind of horse. And she wants six of them." Enza sank into a chair and let her head fall back. "Can you imagine six palominos? That's a lot of horseshit down Main Street. I bet Basking Ridge isn't going to want to give us a permit for that one."

Jo came out of her office and followed her, picked up the trail of dropped belongings and set them on the table. The former living room was a comfortable lounge, furnished with cushy chairs and a few low tables, perfect for greeting clients and brainstorming ideas.

"I don't know," she said soothingly. "There are all kinds of horse people down there."

"And she wants lilacs. She doesn't understand why we can't get lilacs in September. She wants purple and white lilacs for a friggin' fall wedding. She wants the centerpieces to be shallow crystal bowls, surrounded by lilac blossoms, with floating candles."

"That sounds lovely," Jo said.

"Excuse me?" Enza said, her voice raising an octave. "Lilacs? In September?"

Jo picked up Enza's foot and eased off the bright red stiletto. "If you wore regular shoes at these meetings, you'd feel better."

"At least the dress is in and alterations are set. Tuxes taken care of. Venue and menu set. Church booked. What else?" Enza jiggled off the second stiletto and wriggled her toes gratefully.

Jo sat opposite her and frowned, thinking. "Band booked. Harpist booked. Bridesmaids dresses?"

Enza shook her head. "Those girls can't decide what color the sky is on any given day. I told Vienna she had four weeks, or those girls would be wearing push-up bras and thongs as they walked down the aisle."

"Phyl worked out a menu for the McGowan party," Jo said.

Enza raised an eyebrow. "You mean the tea party in the third circle of hell?"

Jo tried not to laugh but failed. "I can only imagine what that old lady is like. Phyl always finds the best in people, no matter how awful they are, and even she had a hard time finding good things to say about Molly McGowan."

"I bet all that gluten-free and sugar-free jacked up the price."

"It did, but Faith McGowan didn't seem to mind."

"Faith McGowan must love her husband to pieces, that's all I gotta say about her. Molly is lucky she hasn't been poisoned in her sleep. By the way, you'll be spending most of that morning picking out all the tomato seeds."

Jo nodded. "So I've been told. No problem. I found a band that plays authentic Irish music, rented the tents, just in case, and the tables, and even found silver tea services."

"That was fast."

"I told you it was going to be easy."

"Ya think? Wait until you get there, start setting up the tables, and that old bat comes out and starts telling you to move them because she's allergic to a particular kind of grass."

Jo laughed again. "We have that retirement thing tomorrow, but it's all set."

"Now, there's a client for you. Easy, understanding, with lots of blank checks. Why can't they all be like that?"

Jo got up and nudged her partner's bare feet. "Yeah, well, then what would you have to complain about?"

"My smart-ass partner?"

"I'm going home. Phyl left. Go on upstairs, soak in a tub and think good thoughts about your fellow man." Jo left the room, took a few minutes to gather her things from her office, and left, locking the front door behind her. Enza took a few deep breaths, got up and headed upstairs.

ENZA LOVED LIVING in her little row house. The home's original kitchen, tiny but adequate, was tucked behind all the office space on the first floor. Enza rarely used it because she rarely cooked. She ate take-out or leftovers from whatever was in the walk-in refrigerators downstairs. She used the second-floor rooms as living space and a guest room and bath for when her daughter flew in from Montana to visit. She converted the entire third floor into her retreat, complete with a king-sized bed, 65-inch-HDTV, and enough closet space for all four of her seasonal wardrobes, plus shoes.

It was there she always headed, at the end of the day, careful to put her clothes away and tuck her shoes in the proper cubbyhole. Her tub was the original claw foot that had been there when she bought the place, and she filled it with hot water and bath salts, put on the classic opera she had listened to with her father, and let the day fade away.

But some days were harder to get through than others.

"Friggin' palominos," she said, slipping into the tub. "How the hell am I going to find six palominos?" She sank into the water and inhaled the faint lavender scent. "Lilacs." She shrugged her shoulders and sank deeper in the water. "Lactose intolerant."

Twenty minutes later, wrapped in a towel and barefoot, she padded downstairs to her kitchen and opened the fridge.

It held six containers from various take-out restaurants, a gallon of half-and-half for her coffee, a wrinkled grapefruit and six bottles of white wine.

"Dinner," she sighed.

She put King Pao chicken in the microwave and opened the wine. She sipped slowly, watching the carousel in the microwave go around. "Irish butter," she muttered. "Lilacs." She finished her glass with a gulp and poured another.

The chicken was hot, and she ate it sitting on a stool by the counter. The original dining room still held a large dining table and chairs, but it was covered in files and neat stacks of papers. Most of the billing was done there, so Enza sat huddled by the counter, fork in one hand, wine glass in the other.

"Lilacs. I'll give her lilacs," she said to herself as she poured a third glass.

The dish and fork went into the dishwasher, the cardboard container into recycling and the bottle with the remaining wine went upstairs.

"Floating candles," she whispered as she fell asleep. "And lilacs."

2

The week of the McGowan tea party began under a cloud. Literally. Monday morning, Enza woke to the sound of thunder, and a quick look at the Weather Channel showed nothing but cartoon clouds and little thunderbolts all week. By the time Jo arrived, Enza was in a state.

"What if it rains on Sunday?" she asked as Jo came through the door.

Jo shook her umbrella and hung up her raincoat, as it was cool for late April. "It's spring, Enza," she soothed. "The weather can change on a dime. Don't worry."

"The Weather Channel says it's going to rain all week."

"The Weather Channel has been known to be wrong."

Enza made a quick motion with her fingers, the traditional gesture guaranteed to keep away evil spirits. "Don't let the cable gods hear you say that," she said darkly. "I can't even imagine, after all this, moving the party indoors. That witch will think it's all Faith's fault." In the days following the meeting at the McGowan house, Enza had exchanged a few emails with Faith, and even spoke a few times on the phone to finalize the menu. She had come to like the quiet, poised woman, and had gone from a neutral party to staunchly Team Faith.

Jo, now used to Enza's shifts in loyalty, shook her head as she followed her partner into the living room. "It's not going to rain on Sunday. And if it does, we have tents, remember? Now, do you seriously think that little old lady is going to blame her daughter-in-law?"

"If God himself came down and called up another flood, she'd blame her daughter-in-law," Enza insisted.

Phyl, who had struggled with the menu for days before finalizing it to Molly's strict guidelines, was leaning Team Faith. "She probably would," she agreed. "I'm sure the son can do no wrong, but his poor wife..."

Jo settled her hands on her hips and glared at her partners. "We do not get personal about our clients," she scolded. "You know that."

"Yeah, well, Molly isn't the client, so I'm going to get as personal as I want," Enza huffed.

That Sunday, however, dawned in a blaze of sunshine. Phyl and Jo loaded up the two white panel Luxe vans with food, silver tea services, and two assistants wearing starched white jackets with the distinctive blue Luxe name on the pocket.

Enza arrived at the McGowan house a few minutes after Jo and Phyl, parked her little black Mercedes around the corner and walked back up the long driveway on sky-high heels. At five foot five, she stood about six inches shorter than she wanted to be. She took the extra height wherever she could find it, no matter how uncomfortable.

The rental company had also just arrived, and Jo was in the back yard directing them as they set up the tables and chairs with their usual efficiency. Enza watched for a few minutes, then headed into the house.

Molly was sitting in a high stool at one end of the huge kitchen island and watched as Phyl and her helpers unpacked food from large plastic bins. "Did you make all this yourself, then?" she asked.

Phyl, her usual smile pasted on her face, nodded. "Of course. Everything today will be homemade."

"Except the tea," Molly cackled. "And the butter. Unless you churn your own butter?"

Phyl still smiled. "No, of course I don't churn me—my own butter. I meant..."

"Mrs. McGowan knows just what you meant," Enza cut in. She stood next to the old woman and glared. "You leave my staff alone, you hear? Or I will have someone carry you upstairs and take away your cane. Got it?"

Molly glared back, saw not an inch of retreat, and sniffed. "My room is on the first floor here," she sniffed. "But...best behavior."

Enza got in a little closer and leaned over the woman. "Damn straight." She straightened. "Where's Faith?"

Molly jerked her head toward the end of the kitchen. "I believe she's having a bit of together time with me son."

At the end of the kitchen, separated by a half-wall, was a little breakfast nook, with floor-to-ceiling windows, a small table, and just two chairs. There were a pair of doors, catty-corner to each other. Enza knocked gently on one, then opened it slowly and peeked in. It was a bathroom, rather large, with another doorway that led outside, obviously for use by the pool. Perfect, she thought. She'd tell everyone this was where to send people who asked. She turned and knocked on the second door and heard a muffled "Come in."

The room looked to be a den or library, with a wall of bookshelves, two comfortable-looking chairs in front of a wide window that overlooked the side yard, and large-screen television. Faith was there, reading the newspaper. The man with her rose and held out a hand.

"I'm Richard. A pleasure to meet you at last. It looks like you're going to give my mother *quite* a day."

Enza shook his hand and understood why any woman would put up with a tiger like Molly. While Faith was pleasantly attractive, Richard McGowan was drop-dead gorgeous, with a head of thick, dark hair just gray at the temples, blue eyes, and the kind of black Irish good looks that were usually found on the covers of romance novels. He also dripped charm. In a few short words, he made Enza feel like she was doing the most important job in the world, and he would be forever in her debt. Any man who could make a woman feel that special, Enza thought, was worth anything. Even Molly.

Enza reined in her natural instinct to flirt. "Well, you have *quite* a mother."

He stared for a minute, then laughed. "Yes, I do. You're right, Faith, darling. These ladies can handle her just fine." He stepped back. "I hope you'll understand that Faith and I will probably be hanging out here for most of the day. I want Mother to enjoy this time with her friends."

"Of course." She thought about the comment Jo had made weeks ago about the client spending the day drinking vodka martinis. She felt a pang of envy. "Can I join you?"

He laughed again, and this time Faith joined him.

"Once all the guests have arrived, we're probably going to lock ourselves in here," Faith said. "With so many people around, we don't want just anyone wandering in. But the secret password is Sanctuary."

Richard leaned over and kissed the top of his wife's head. "Ah, darling, I'm so sorry that Sanctuary is what you need right now. But I understand perfectly."

Enza laughed and shut the door behind her, wondering where in the world she could find another Richard McGowan.

ENZA WENT BACK into the kitchen and found Jo nose to nose with Molly McGowan.

"I said I wanted real silverware," Molly was saying, her face red.

Jo Collins was a tiny woman and looked much younger than her thirty-three years. Barely five feet tall, and possibly ninety pounds, she did have a great deal of attitude, and at the moment it was erupting from her pores.

"And you have silverware. But no, you do not have *sterling* silverware because, although we are calling this a high tea, this is not Buckingham Palace and you are *not* the Queen."

Molly stiffened her back. "I bet if I stabbed someone with a fork, that cheap thing would bend in half."

Jo, who was, in that moment, holding a fork, held it up to Molly's nose. "Want me to test your theory?"

Enza hurried over, gently removed the fork from Jo's hand, and shouldered her way in front of Molly. "Now, really, what did we just talk about?" She pushed back with her butt, creating a few more valuable inches between Jo and Molly. "Best behavior, remember?"

"I'll not have this little chit of a girl lyin' to me face."

"Jo wouldn't lie. Ever."

"She's trying to tell me that chintzy bit right there is

silverware, and I can see from across the room it's that awful stainless steel."

"Mrs. McGowan," Enza said gently, "surely you must have known we wouldn't have real *silver* silverware."

Molly leaned toward Enza. "It's what I asked for. And it's what you promised."

"Well, that's where the misunderstanding is. You see, you asked for real silver, not real *silverware*, so I thought you meant silver *serving* pieces. Jo, why don't you run out and get one of those gorgeous teapots for Mrs. McGowan here?"

Molly opened her mouth, frowned, and gave Enza a long look. "Caught me on a technicality," she said.

"Whatever I can get, Mrs. McGowan."

When Jo came back, her face was no longer the same color as her hair. She handed the teapot to Molly who immediately flipped it over to read the mark on the bottom. She made a huffy kind of a noise, raised her eyebrows in the closest she'd come to submission in decades, and handed it back. "I suppose."

"Yes, well." Enza put her hands on Jo's shoulders, turned the younger woman around, and pushed her back toward the patio. "Why don't we let Jo get back to work? And Phyl, things here fine?"

Phyl had been watching, her eyes practically falling out of her head. Her assistants, Gina and Laurel, still had their mouths hanging open.

"We're good," Phyl said. She glanced back at her two girls and made a motion with her head. "Work, you two. Get to it."

The girls scurried back to the end of the counter.

"You know, Mrs. McGowan," Enza said, easing the old lady off the stool. "And can I call you Molly?"

"No."

"Fine. You know, Molly, we've got at least another hour of set-up here, and if you see everything that's going on, that will kill all the surprise. Don't you want to have something to look forward too?"

"No."

"Yes. Well, you're going to. Why don't you sit in the living room? Or better yet, look, the band just got here. Want to sit outside and listen to them warm up?"

Something lit up in Molly's eyes that was not vicious or hateful, but rather, delighted. The band had indeed arrived, five men carrying unrecognizable, to Enza at least, bundles that obviously held instruments.

"Will ye look at that," Molly said softly. "He's got an accordion. And...a bouzouki. Bless my soul, a bouzouki."

Enza had no idea what a bouzouki was, nor did she care. Molly walked slowly through the French doors, cane thumping, out across the patio, and followed the musicians to the large, leafy maple.

"Oh, thank you, Jesus," Enza said reverently. She looked back. Gina and Laurel burst into giggles, and Phyl buried her head in her hands.

"That food better be perfect," she warned. "Or I'll give Molly your home addresses."

The girls laughed harder, and Phyl lifted her head, her face wet with tears. "Enza, you're a miracle worker," she said through her laughter.

Enza smiled to herself and followed Molly outside.

Jo was talking to a short, balding man who was trying to listen to her while not ignoring Molly, who seemed to have an awful lot to say. Enza hurried over as fast as she could on her heels, eager to separate Jo and Molly as soon as possible.

"Jo, honey," she said, "Let me deal with Mr...."

"Lloyd," the man said. "Please, call me Lloyd."

Jo practically ran in the other direction as Enza tried to shut out Molly's voice.

"Lloyd, this is our guest of honor," Enza said loudly. "Mrs. Molly McGowan. It's her birthday we're celebrating today."

He had to look up at her and appeared to be concentrating hard on what she was saying. Enza could understand his dilemma; Molly was telling him about her days in London and a particular pub that featured a particular band that sang a particular song...

He then turned to Molly, took her hand, bowed and kissed it. "Mrs. McGowan, I tell you it's an absolute honor to be here to perform for you for such as auspicious occasion." His hair was as gray and thinning with the strands carefully spread for maximum coverage across his scalp. His accent was thick, and there was a charming lilt to his voice. "I can tell that you are a woman of strong opinions, which is something I admire greatly. If you'll just let me help the boys?"

Molly blushed. "Of course, Lloyd. Sorry."

Enza stared at Molly, then at Lloyd. Was he, in fact, one of the Irish fairies she had read about as a child? Because to extract an apology from Molly was nothing short of magical.

Lloyd grinned, showing small, white teeth, and hurried back to the circle of men under the maple. Enza took a step after him. What, exactly, was an Irish band anyway? She'd been raised on opera, then disco, then punk rock. There were four of them in a huddle, all looking to be whatever age Lloyd was— around sixty— and all of them dressed in baggy trousers, button-down shirts and vests. They also seemed uniformly short. And then the fifth man, who had been kneeling on the ground opening his guitar case, stood up. He looked to be at least a foot taller than his fellow musicians and decidedly younger. Enza took a few steps closer.

His hair was dark, almost blue-black, thick, and rather long, falling across his high forehead. His body was lean, and his shirtsleeves were rolled to the elbow, showing strong and decidedly sexy forearms. Enza took one more step, and he strummed a few chords. She was torn between watching his fingers as they danced across the strings, and looking at his face, half-hidden by the fall of his hair. Then, he lifted his head, looked right at her, and she almost fell off her three-inch heels.

His smile dazzled. "Any requests?" he asked her.

She began to make a list. Take off your shirt, peel off those jeans, dive into the pool, pull yourself out with those amazing arms, walk toward me soaking wet and dripping...

"Cry For Love," she said.

His eyebrows shot up and his smile broadened. "A woman after my own heart," he said, and his fingers began to work, and she recognized the familiar melody at once.

One of the other men looked over. "Now, Connor," he called good-naturedly, "stick to the playlist."

Enza's heart raced even faster. Tall, dark, handsome, played Iggy Pop, and his name was *Connor*?

Connor stopped playing, shrugged and looked apologetic. "Sorry. Gotta stick with the guys, here." He took a few steps toward her, his guitar hanging by his side. "But maybe, during our break, we can have an Iggy-fest? You and me?"

Enza immediately started calculating where this could possibly go. She automatically assumed that, if she wanted, she could have him. It wasn't ego that made her think that way, but rather years of experience. There was something about her that men liked and liked a lot. Although she rarely used it, she knew it was there and called on it whenever she felt the need. Like right now.

She was probably older than him, although not by much. He was a musician, which appealed to the romantic in her. She also found him very attractive. Not all women liked long, lean and a bit craggy, so maybe he wasn't used to picking up women at every gig. She wasn't looking at him as a long-term partner. She was very happy in her singlehood and gave no serious thought to finding another man to settle down with. But for a bit of a fling...

"Connor, I'd be more than happy to Iggy with you." She looked up at him and gave him a smile. "I'm Enza."

He took her hand and held it. "I'm delighted."

"Darlin'," one of the men called out to her, "I need to tell you. We have to watch Connor like a hawk, or he'd be off behind the bushes with someone at every gig. Not that any of them complain, mind."

She raised an eyebrow. "No complaints? *Ever*? Well, that's good, at least."

He didn't even blush, just threw back his head and laughed. "They're just jealous," he said loudly enough for the rest of the band to hear, "because I'm the only one here who can still get it up at all."

The men all laughed, and Enza joined them. "I will certainly keep your invitation in mind," she said to Connor. "But since I'm running this little party, I may not get a break."

He leaned down to whisper in her ear. "Then we'll have to work something else out, right?"

She looked up at him through her eyelashes. Her heart was pounding so hard she was sure he could hear it, but she kept her voice calm and cool. "We'll see," she said, and turned and walked away, striding gracefully across the grass, all the time praying she did not fall off her shoes, twist an ankle, run into the edge of a table, fall into the pool...

She glanced back. Connor was back under the tree. Molly was sitting down in the sun, watching the band as they started tuning their instruments. Enza looked around. The sun was shining and the tables were all set. Each of the five round tables looked lovely, with crisp white linen, pale pink tableware, and white lilies in glass vases in the center of each. The stainless flatware gleamed in the sun.

It was party time. And everything was perfect.

And then the heel of her shoe, two out of the three inches of it, sank into the ground, and as she took a step, her foot came out of it completely. She wobbled, tried to step back, and the other heel became equally stuck. She stumbled, almost falling, a few feet forward, and then stood, eyes closed, hoping no one had seen, wondering how she could gracefully turn around and yank her wayward high heels out of the McGowan's perfectly mown lawn...

"Enza?"

She turned. Connor was there, holding both of her shoes. His clear blue eyes were dancing, but he was managing to keep a straight face.

She cleared her throat. "Thank you," she said, took the shoes and walked, barefoot, back into the house.

ENZA HAD ASSUMED that most of the attendees of Molly McGowan's seventieth birthday party would have been, if not her exact age, at least her generation. While a few of the ladies that came in looked and, for those with walkers, acted like a pre-baby boomer, most of the guests were much younger than Molly. And there were quite a few men. No one at Luxe had addressed the invitations—there was a service that did all that—so Enza was surprised by the age, sex, and variety of physical dexterity that came through the front door.

Molly and Richard greeted each guest. Faith stood back, just inside the kitchen doorway, and mumbled in Enza's ear as each guest made their way to the back yard.

"That's Helen somebody. Older than dirt. Was Molly's maid of honor or something."

Enza did not ask what Faith was drinking. It was clear and iced. That was all she knew and that's all she cared to know.

"That guy there? We think he was giving her a little of the old whatever back in the late eighties. He's got to be ten, maybe fifteen years younger than she is. Can you imagine?"

Enza, quite truthfully, could not.

"And look at that. My sister. God, I hate my family."

Faith's sister looked just like Faith, but her features were sharper, her hair a bit brighter, make-up more pronounced. She kissed Molly at the front door, shook Richard's hand, and as she made her way to the back of the house, stopped and stared at Faith.

Faith raised her voice. "Linda," she said, her voice flat. "Imagine you being here."

Linda narrowed her eyes and glanced back at Molly and Richard, who were busy with a rather well-dressed man, decidedly younger than Molly.

"That's her banker if you can believe it," Faith muttered. "She invited the money-man? I didn't think she even liked him—and—oh God, is she really coming over here?"

Faith immediately smiled brightly as Linda grew close. "Linda, dear, this is Enza. She put this party together for Mother. And I must say, the whole thing is quite marvelous."

Linda glanced at Enza. "Yes. Quite. I can't understand why you didn't organize this, Faith. You're so good at this sort of thing."

"As well as you know my mother-in-law, I would have thought you'd understand perfectly."

They nodded to each other and Linda moved away.

Enza took a breath. The level of drama was getting ridiculous. What could top this? Then—

"Oh, that woman," Faith whispered.

Enza looked over. Faith's eyes were full of tears and her chin was trembling. Enza took a step closer.

"Faith?"

Faith gave her head a quick shake. "She invited Virginia Crewe. What a spiteful old woman." Enza watched as Faith took several deep breaths and blinked away tears.

"Who's Virginia Crewe?" Enza asked in a whisper.

"The woman Richard was engaged to when he met me," Faith explained in a quavering voice. "Molly was furious when he broke it off to marry me, and she's never gotten over it. Neither has Virginia. The woman is deranged. She once followed me to work and..." Faith shook her head. "Never mind. But trust Molly to find a way to twist the knife, even now."

Enza looked over to see Molly embrace a tiny, frail-looking woman with pale blonde hair and a thin, stooped figure, wearing a demure beige suit with a colorful purple scarf around her neck. She saw Molly shoot Faith a smug look over the woman's shoulder. Richard, for the first time, looked uncomfortable as he greeted his ex-flame, but his smile never wavered.

While Enza had been perfectly happy to stand next to Faith and get the dirt on the guests, she had no interest in being that close to a family squabble. She excused herself and moved to the other side of the kitchen counter, where Phyl was placing tiny mint leaves on the tops of flakey pastry cups filled with thinly sliced strawberries, kiwi fruit, and mango.

"They look gorgeous," Enza said. "Are they going out first?"

Phyl nodded. She had managed to get old-fashioned silver and china servers, three tiers high, several for each of the five tables. One would be for the fruit and cheese puffs, one for savory sandwiches, one for plain scones, and one for the sweets. They would be placed on each table, along with the tea and hot cocoa, as well as crystal pitchers of cold pink lemonade, and taken back into the kitchen to refill as needed.

Gina and Laurel were carefully arranging the puffs on the servers. Enza reached for one, only to have her hand slapped.

"Don't you dare," Phyl said. "I know we're going to run out. I just know it."

Enza rolled her eyes and Gina and Laurel giggled. Phyl lived in constant fear of having her clients slowly die of starvation because of her miscalculations.

"Gluten-free?" Enza asked.

Phyl nodded. Enza headed for the back yard.

The guests were mingling happily, checking out the place cards, making small talk. The band was playing softly, something very sweet and vaguely familiar. She stole a glance at Connor, who must have been watching her because he immediately caught her eye and grinned. She felt heat rising to her face, and she began to brush off tiny bits of flotsam that had fallen from the trees on to the starched white tablecloth.

Jo came up behind her. "Are you making eyes at that

very hot guitar player?"

Enza moved a fork an eighth of an inch to the left. "What very hot guitar player?"

Jo snorted and moved on.

Enza retreated as the last of the guests came out, and people began to find their seats. Laurel and Gina would be in charge of serving four of the tables. Jo was dedicating herself to Molly's table. Enza would move between outside and Phyl in the kitchens.

They had done this before. They had it down to a science. Enza caught Jo's eye and grinned.

They had this.

Technically speaking, the party ended at five o'clock. The McGowan's and Luxe had both agreed that two hours was enough time to serve tea, sit in the sun, and celebrate a stately seventieth birthday.

Enza, after having met Molly, should have known better.

At some point, Molly started filling her water glass with something that looked very much like whiskey, completely ignoring the carefully prepared lactose-and-sugar-free hot chocolate that Phyl had dutifully brewed in a large stock-pot. Whatever Molly had started drinking quickly spread. Enza had never seen so many silver flasks in one place at one time in her life. After a bit of encouragement, the band went from soothing Irish ballads to rousing dance tunes, and Molly began pulling people out of their chairs to dance.

Jo, her blazing red hair piled up on the top of her head, in her Luxe white jacket and sensible walking shoes, nodded her head and tapped her foot in time to the music.

"These guys are really good," Jo said as she and Enza

stood, poolside, and watched as Molly's quiet and dignified high tea turned into something quite different.

Enza, who watched Connor as he strummed his guitar and stomped his foot to the music, nodded in agreement. "They may be the best Irish band I've ever heard."

Jo poked Enza with her elbow. "I bet this is the *only* Irish band you've ever heard."

Connor looked around, caught Enza staring, and grinned at her again. She was having little heart palpitations. This party needed to be over, so she could find a quiet little corner somewhere and find out what else Connor could do with those long, beautiful fingers.

"How can a woman who needs a cane to walk," Enza mused, "dance like that in her bare feet? Look at those steps!"

Molly smiled broadly and moved with surprising grace in a small circle of admirers who clapped and urged her on. As the music got faster, so did her feet, until she finally threw up her hands and threw her arms around Linda, Faith's sister, who patted the old lady on the back and helped her back to her chair.

"This needs to end soon," Jo said, checking her watch. "The rental company will be here to start taking away the tables and chairs."

Enza shook her head as she watched Molly's guests pair off to dance some sort of reel to yet another fast, catchy Irish tune. "Are you going to tell them?"

Phyl came up behind them, wiping her hands on her apron. "I knew it. I am running out of food," she said.

"This party was over twenty minutes ago," Enza said. "Our obligation to feed them is now over. Let's get the girls to start clearing the tables."

The food and extras that Luxe used were taken to and

from the vans on specially designed carts. Enza went into the kitchen to see how much was left to pack and noticed the door to the den standing open. She walked over, thinking she'd stick her head in just to see how Faith was faring but froze in the doorway.

Faith and Virginia Crewe were standing so close they were almost touching, their voices high-pitched and getting louder.

"...were never good enough for him, and we both know it," Virginia hissed. She was about six inches shorter than Faith, and the muscles on her neck were bulging as she stared upwards.

"He made his choice because you were a manipulative madwoman and he couldn't take your constant demands any longer. If he'd never met me, he still would have thrown you to the curb," Faith shot back.

"You took all of this away from me," Virginia wailed. "This should have been my life.'

"You've had over thirty years to create your own life, Ginny. Instead, you chose to sit back and mourn what was never yours to begin with. Now, get out."

Virginia Crewe stood up on her toes and tried to push Faith a step back, but Faith grabbed Virginia by the shoulders and gave her a shove.

"Faith?" Enza called sharply. "Are you all right?"

Faith turned to Enza, her eyes blazing. "Get this woman away from me."

Enza hurried in and took Virginia by the arm, drawing her away. "Let's get back outside," she said to Virginia. Behind her, she heard the door shut, and a small click.

The older woman was shaking and in tears. "Did you see that? She struck me. She was always a thug. All her airs, and she's still just a street bitch."

"Maybe," Enza said, pulling harder, "but it's her house."

Virginia clawed at the scarf around her neck, hands trembling. "Do you see this here?" she said, waving her hand toward the room, her voice high and quivering. "This should have been mine. This would have been mine except for that woman."

Enza shook her head. "You mean except for Richard, don't you? Didn't he make the final decision?"

Virginia froze, narrowed her eyes and stormed through the kitchen, past a confused-looking Jo.

"What?" Jo asked.

Enza shook her head. "No more little old ladies," Enza muttered. "I'll tell you later." Enza and Jo went out front and wheeled the carts from the vans directly on to the patio, then into the kitchen. They loaded the carts and wheeled them back out to the van. As she came around from the second trip, Enza saw Richard standing poolside with Phyl, talking.

"Looks like it was a huge success," Enza said to Richard.

He turned to her, a huge smile on his face. "Yes, look at them! I haven't seen my mother this happy in years. I almost hate to break this up."

Gina and Laurel were clearing the tables, one at a time, and putting everything directly into the plastic bins that were then fitted onto the carts. They had cleared two of the five tables, packing the dirty plates and cutlery, and piling the linen in the center of the bare tables. The guests did not take the hint. They simply moved the folding chairs and crowded the remaining tables.

"It's after six. The rental people will be here soon," Enza said to Richard. "What should we do?"

Richard looked around. "Maybe we should tell the band to quit playing?"

Jo moved, waving until she caught Lloyd's eye, and made a motion under her throat—cut. Lloyd nodded, and at the end of the song, the band relaxed and lowered their instruments.

There was a sound of displeasure from the crowd. Molly, once again sitting, waved her cane.

"Richard, tell them to keep playing," she called. "Good Lord knows you've got the money for it."

There was scattered laughter, but Richard shook his head. "Party's over folks. Sorry."

Phyl sighed. "There's nothing in the kitchen except empty bowls and trays. I believe there may be scones left, but I'm sure they're not in very good shape."

Enza put her arm around her partner and gave a squeeze. "This, my friend, is something you can be proud of. Given what you *couldn't* work with, it was an unqualified success. Jo and I cleared most of the kitchen, but let's get the last, okay?"

They headed back in, each carrying an empty bin. They neatly stacked the serving pieces that were left in just minutes, and Enza saw that Phyl was right, there was nothing left of all the food Luxe had brought, except a tray of scones that Phyl wrapped and left on the counter.

"I'll grab a cart," Enza said. "These bins weigh a friggin' ton."

Richard had moved from in front of the pool off to the side and was half-hidden in the bushes, but Enza heard his voice clearly as she stepped outside. Gone was the calm, cultured voice that had greeted guests and chatted earlier. He sounded furious.

"...don't want to go over this again," he argued. "You're in this just as deep."

Enza paused and strained to hear. Richard's back was to

her, and she could see he was talking to the man Faith had pointed out earlier, Molly's banker.

"Listen, Richard, calm down." The banker didn't sound too happy either, but he was keeping his voice steady. "I'm on board. You know that."

"And as long as we all keep our mouths shut, no one will know," Richard said, his voice low and shaking. "Now get the hell away from me and do your job."

Enza ducked her head and trotted past, grabbed one of the half-filled carts, and pushed it toward the kitchen.

Richard passed her, his handsome face flushed. Enza steered the cart to the open French doors and she and Phyl loaded the last two heavy bins. Then, they began to push the cart off the patio to the driveway, where both vans had parked.

"This looks heavy," a voice behind them said. "Can I help?"

It was Connor, and he stepped between Enza and Phyl and pushed the cart effortlessly to the drive and up the ramp, into the van. "Anything else I can do for you?" he asked.

Phyl sighed and smiled. "No, but thank you so much. And thanks also for that lovely music. Wasn't it wonderful, Enza?"

Enza was looking up into those blue eyes. Even in her heels, she had to tilt her head. "Wonderful," she agreed. He began to walk with them back toward the house.

"Now, have you always been a musician?" Phyl asked.

He nodded his head. "Yes. My first band was in the sixth grade."

"Imagine that! Why, you must be very good at your job," Phyl said.

He chuckled. "This is a side gig, and even though I've

been playing most of my life, the boys still tell me every time not to give up my day job." He was looking at Phyl as he spoke to her but turned to flash a grin at Enza.

How on earth was she going to get this man alone for even five minutes? Phyl had a genuine interest in people, and if she found Connor worthy, she could spend the rest of the day with him, asking endless questions.

On the patio, he stopped, put both his hands on his hips, and looked over to where his bandmates were almost done packing their instruments. Enza was far enough behind him to admire the rather outstanding view without having to twist her head too much. "Phyl," she said, "I see Gina and Laurel. Can you find Jo for me? The rental truck should be here any minute. Could you check the kitchen?"

Phyl smiled again up at Connor. "Again, thank you, and it was a real pleasure."

Enza watched her as she walked off, then turned to Connor. "We never got to Iggy," she said.

"Well, the day isn't over, now, is it?" He nodded at his bandmates. They were packing up, except for Lloyd, who was in deep conversation with Molly. "We should be packed up and ready to go soon. How long before you wrap the rest of this up?"

She shrugged. "The rental guys are due at seven, any minute now, and as soon as they're done, we're done."

"There's a pub in Montclair, Lyons, do you know it?"

"No," she said, smiling. "But that's what a GPS is for."

He smiled back. "We could meet there, in, say an hour? Get a drink? Maybe a bite to eat? If you get me drunk enough, I may tell you my darkest secrets."

She took a step closer. "And just how dark *are* they?"

"Ah, now," he shook his head and made a clucking noise.

"That would be telling." He leaned down to whisper. "And it's much more fun to show, don't you think?"

She felt an actual tingle right in her stomach that burned for a second, then headed south. "That sounds almost wicked."

He grinned. "Let's hope."

And then there was a scream from the house.

Enza's head turned. There was another scream, a different voice. And then two screams together.

She ran, following Connor into the house.

Phyl and Jo stood together at the end of the kitchen, in the breakfast nook, arms wrapped around each other.

"What?" Enza called sharply.

Phyl pointed through the open door to the den.

Enza came into the room right behind Connor, who stopped abruptly and put out an arm to keep her from going in any farther, but she saw what he saw. Faith McGowan, sitting in her armchair, the newspaper spread across her chest, head back and eyes wide open.

"Is she dead?" Phyl asked.

Connor crossed the room in two long strides and knelt beside Faith, laying a finger against the side of her neck. "Call 911," he said, but Enza already had the phone out.

She went back into the kitchen and pushed Phyl and Jo away from the doorway. She took Jo's arm and gave it a shake. "Go outside. Close the doors behind you. Don't let anyone in. Okay?"

Jo nodded, eyes wide, and she took Phyl with her.

"911. What is your emergency?"

Enza looked back into the den. Connor met her eye and shook his head.

"Someone has died," Enza said. "We need an ambulance." She gave the address and clicked off the phone.

"Did she have a heart attack?" she asked in a hushed voice.

Connor rolled down the sleeve of his shirt, and, covering his hand with the cuff, he lifted the newspaper. Enza could see the hilt of a knife. The newspaper dropped.

"Faith?" Richard pushed his way past Enza. "Faith?"

Connor stood and blocked Richard from coming closer. "I'm sorry, but we need to leave this room. We can't touch anything."

"What?" Richard croaked. "That's my wife. This is my house."

"I'm sorry," Connor said softly. "But she's dead. And this is now a crime scene."

Enza took Richard's arm and led him away as he began to wail.

3

———

Two police cars arrived at the same time as the crew from the rental company. The officers issued the same order to everyone—don't touch anything, and don't leave.

Most of the guests had left before Phyl and Jo had discovered Faith's body, but there were a handful of people left, sitting under the umbrellas, looking dazed. Molly was sitting with Richard in the living room. The band members were under the maple tree, except for Connor, who met the police and led them inside the house. The ladies from Luxe huddled poolside, Gina still sniffling. Enza broke away from them when the police arrived and followed them back into the house.

Connor had somehow gone from a lanky and carefree musician to a well informed and unshaken witness. Enza watched him carefully. He knew about police procedure. He had all the answers to the questions the police were asking. He was talking to one officer with an attitude that led Enza to believe he'd done this sort of thing before. What kind of day job does a guitar player have that makes him so comfortable around dead bodies?

He turned at the sound of sirens and caught sight of her. He spoke briefly to the police officer, then hurried over to her, taking her by the arm and leading her outside.

"Are you okay? Shouldn't you be sitting down? This has to be a shock for you." The concern in his voice sounded real.

Enza nodded. "Yes, it is. I don't see dead people every day. But you do, right?"

He stopped and exhaled loudly.

"Are you a cop?" she asked.

He shook his head. "No. Well, yes. I'm a special investigator with the FBI."

"A Fed?"

He nodded.

"Who moonlights with an Irish band on the weekends?"

He shrugged. "Not every weekend. Sometimes I'm on assignment." He looked at her and his mouth twisted. "Not so much fun anymore, is it?"

She poked his chest with her manicured index finger. "Connor, you only say that because you don't know me very well. Yet."

He raised an eyebrow. "Really?"

She squeezed his upper arm with both hands. "But you're right. I'm in shock. Don't be surprised if I feel the need to hold on to you for physical and emotional support."

He looked toward the house. "Then we'd better get back inside. The detectives should be here."

They went back into the kitchen. There were more uniformed officers, as well as two men in dark suits, one of which looked up as they entered.

"Connor? Jeez, what are you doing here?"

Connor shook his hand. "Coincidence, believe me. How are you, Mike?"

"Good." The detective looked past Connor to Enza. "Your assistant?"

Connor shook his head. "She organized the party. Enza, this is Detective Mike Whalen." He held out his hand to the second detective. "Connor Ives. FBI."

The second detective shook his hand. "Jack Newberry. What have we got?"

"Birthday party gone bad," Connor said. "Body was found about fifteen minutes ago. I don't think she's been dead long. The body was still warm."

Detective Whalen nodded. "Yeah, we just looked. They used a kitchen knife. Whoever did this was taking a real risk with so many people around."

"Most everyone was outside," Enza said. "The kitchen was probably empty for a while."

Mike looked at her closely. "Someone followed her in from outside?"

Enza shook her head. "Mrs. McGowan did not come out at all. She spent the afternoon right in that room, most of the time with her husband."

Whalen raised an eyebrow. "Not the party type?"

"Not this party." Enza frowned, thinking. "At five, Richard came out. The husband. They'd been in there together through most of the party. My crew left the kitchen a few minutes after that."

Whalen stopped taking notes. "Your crew? How many?"

"My two partners are here, and two helpers," she said. "I saw Faith, around five-fifteen. She and Virginia Crewe were having a ...discussion. I left her in the den. That was the last time I saw her alive. We were all out of the kitchen by, say five-thirty. We cleared the tables and started to try to get people out of here. Maybe an hour later, Phyl—my partner — and I were back in the kitchen, loading our carts to take out to the van. Connor helped us. Figure that took another, what, ten minutes? We were walking back. Jo, my other partner, must have gone into the kitchen for a last look around because that's when she and Phyl found Mrs. McGowan. Whoever did this had a few windows of opportunity. First, when Richard came out when the party was just ending, and we were all out clearing tables. Or they could have snuck in and out pretty quickly while we were taking the carts to the van. Or maybe the killer snuck in, heard us, and just waited for us to leave before slipping out. After all, the door was locked from the inside. Or—"

"Enza," Connor said softly in her ear, "why don't we let these gentlemen do their job?"

She looked up at him. "I'm just trying to help. Let's face it, that's a pretty important timeline."

"Yes, it is," Whalen agreed. "We'll need to speak to this Phyl person. And Jo."

Enza nodded. "I'll get them." She stepped away from him, and Connor's attention immediately went back to the detectives. Enza took a few more steps, then sidled into the dining room. She could see into the living room, where Richard sat, his mother next to him on the couch, and Faith's sister, Linda, on a chair across the room.

Linda was dry-eyed and composed, whereas Richard was bent over, his face in his hands, shoulders shaking. Molly had her hand on his back and was speaking quietly to him. She looked up and saw Enza. Her face didn't change, but her eyes narrowed into glittering slits. Enza turned and walked away, went back poolside, and motioned for Phyl and Jo to come in.

.   .   .

45

"DETECTIVE, before we start, can I send away the rental trucks?" Enza asked. "They didn't get here until after Mrs. McGowan was killed, they know nothing, and they're charging me by the hour for parking in the driveway."

They were all sitting around the dining room table. Richard, his mother, and sister-in-law were still in the living room, with two uniformed officers and a few men in plain-clothes. Detectives Whalen and Newberry were across the table from the ladies from Luxe, and Connor leaned against the doorway into the kitchen.

Whalen and Newberry whispered together, both nodded, and Whalen motioned to one of the uniformed cops in the living room.

"Let the rental trucks go," he called.

"Thank you," Enza said.

"Sure," Whalen said. "So, Ms....," he glanced at his notebook. "Collins. You and Ms. Anders found the body?"

Jo nodded. Her perky bun had come undone, and red hair fell around her face. She pushed a strand behind her ear. "We had—"

"Who's we?" Newberry asked.

"Myself, and the two girls who were working the event with us. Gina and Laurel. We'd cleared the tables, stripped the linen, and folded most of the chairs. The birthday girl, that is, Molly McGowan, wasn't budging, and there were about a half dozen people sitting with her, so we took the loaded cart into our van, and I told the girls to just sit and wait. I knew that Enza and Phyl had packed up the kitchen, but we always double-check, so I went in to see if we were all clear."

Newberry nodded encouragingly. "Go on."

"There was nothing of ours left. I used the bathroom, and that's when I noticed that the door to the den was open, just a crack. It had been closed throughout the party, so I thought I'd just peek in and say goodbye." She swallowed hard. "I opened up the door and she was just... there. Her eyes were, like, bugging out. I didn't mean to scream, really, but, I mean...I could kinda tell she was dead."

"What time was this?" asked Whalen.

"Seven? Just before? The rental truck was due here at seven, but those guys always run a little late."

"Then what?"

"Then Phyl was there," Jo said. "I guess she had come in looking for me. She ran to me, took a look, and then *she* screamed."

Phyl, who had put her hands to her mouth and not moved them, spoke through her palms. "She was dead. I could tell. Of course I screamed."

"And then, we both screamed," Jo explained.

"Then Connor and Enza ran in, looked, and Enza told us to leave and make sure no one came in," Phyl said. She brought down her hands from her mouth. "Of course, when Mr. McGowan asked to be let in, we didn't stop him."

Newberry sat back. "You are the party planners?"

The three women nodded.

"So, you've never met any of these people before?" he asked.

Enza spoke. "Phyl and I met with Mrs. McGowan a few weeks before the party. Here. We walked around the house, looked at the kitchen and the outdoor space, and left. All other contact was by phone or email. We all got here around noon today. The rental company set up the tables, chairs, and umbrellas. They also had the linens for the tables. We had everything else. We met with Mr. and Mrs. McGowan briefly, and with the...older Mrs. McGowan. Molly. Mr. and

Mrs. said they would be spending most of the time back in the den."

"Why?" Whalen asked. "If this was his mother's party, wouldn't they have been celebrating with everyone else?"

"Excuse me, but have you *met* Molly McGowan?" Jo blurted.

Whalen and Newberry exchanged glances. "Briefly," Whalen said. "Why?"

"She's a terror," Jo said. "And she hated her daughter-in-law."

Whalen scribbled some more. "And you know this how?"

Enza cleared her throat. "Faith herself told me. But even if she hadn't, it was obvious if you spent more than five minutes in a room with the two of them."

"Well," Whalen said dryly, "that's impossible for us now. So be clearer."

Phyl put her hand to her cheek. "Molly was rude and dismissive in her conversation with poor Faith. She was also incredibly unappreciative of Faith's efforts on her behalf. When you interview her, you'll probably find her rude and dismissive with you as well. Just imagine *living* with it."

Whalen leaned back. "Well, that's a pretty good motive, then, don't you think? Hatred?"

Enza glanced at Jo, and then, because she just wanted to see his face, looked at Connor. His lips were a thin line, and his eyes were half-closed.

"Molly needed a cane," Enza said.

"Except when she was dancing," Jo countered. "She was pretty spry out there earlier."

Whalen closed his notebook. "Please stay here. We need to speak to Mr. McGowan."

"Can we go outside? Please?" Phyl asked, her voice thin and pleading.

Newberry nodded. "Sure."

The three ladies stood, but Enza motioned Jo and Phyl to the door as she crossed over to Connor. "So, what do you think," she asked in a low voice.

He raised an eyebrow. "About what?"

"About who killed Faith McGowan, of course? What else?"

He shook his head. "Enza, this is a police matter. I have no opinion."

Enza rolled her eyes. "Oh, come on. Professional curiosity, right? And you were here the whole time, while it was happening. Don't tell me you're not itching to have a go at this."

He chuckled. "Enza, I happen to be a professional investigator for the Federal Bureau of Investigation, with a Masters and a law degree. I don't get *itchy*."

She stepped closer to him, her rather full breasts barely touching the front of his shirt. She looked up at him. "My mistake," she said softly.

He made a noise in the back of his throat and stepped back, hitting the wall.

She smiled. "I'll be right outside," she said. Then she turned and followed Phyl and Jo out to the pool.

THE MOOD outside of the house was grim. Jo and Phyl had found seats with the remaining guests, four stressed-out looking individuals who were being carefully watched by an officer in uniform. It was getting dark, and the outside house lights were on, as well as the lights around the pool. Faces were in shadows and nobody looked happy. The four remaining band members had put chairs under the maple tree and were talking quietly, passing around a silver flask. Lloyd stood as Enza came across the lawn.

"Has my man Connor made a case for us to go home?" he asked.

She shook her head. "He's out of this, Lloyd. He told me it was a police matter. They make the decisions."

He said something rather nasty sounding, in Gaelic. "What's the use of having a copper in the band if he's no good to you in a pinch?"

"Good question, Lloyd. But I don't have the answer."

She sat down next to Phyl and stared across the table at the forlorn guests. She recognized the gentleman as the banker Richard had argued with earlier. The women looked to be Molly's contemporaries.

"Did any of you all know Faith?" Enza asked.

Jo looked at Enza sharply. "Why are you asking questions?" she asked in a low voice.

"Because I'm curious," Enza replied shortly. "Well?"

The banker cleared his throat. "I've known—knew—Faith for almost fifteen years, ever since she became Molly's trustee."

"Trustee?"

He nodded. "There was a great deal of money, and Richard placed a generous amount in his mother's name some years ago. Faith was the trustee of that money."

Enza pursed her lips. "I bet Molly loved that."

One of the older women made a very rude noise. "That Faith," she said, her accent as thick as Molly's, "made poor Molly explain every single penny spent. Watched her like a hawk, she did. As though Molly wasn't a grown woman, perfectly capable of making her own financial decisions with her own money."

"But it wasn't her money, was it?" Enza asked. "It was Richard's money."

The woman looked taken aback. "But he gave it to her!"

The woman next to her tut-tutted. "Now, Helen, you know that Molly likes her baubles. And she spent an awful lot of money on them." She leaned toward Enza. "I'm Mary-Beth Riley. I've known Molly since Richard was in nappies. We were neighbors, you see. Molly is a great friend and a good woman, but, my, she liked to spend her pennies on shiny things."

Enza, who had not seen one single thing shine on Molly all day, was surprised. "You mean jewelry?"

MaryBeth shook her head. "No. Them little German children."

Phyl frowned. "Children?"

Helen nodded. "Yes. Those figurines. But, the real ones. Antiques."

Jo's eyes popped wide open. "Hummels?"

MaryBeth slapped the top of the table. "That's right. Not the cheap ones you can get online either. She got them from a fancy dealer in New York City, she did. She'd save up for a couple of years, then make the trip in. I went with her once." She dropped her voice. "She spent almost eight thousand dollars that day. On a little boy in a funny hat sitting on a swing."

Enza gave a low whistle. "Those are some baubles."

"And why shouldn't she have them?" the third woman piped up. "She worked her whole life for that boy. She deserved a few nice things in her old age."

Helen tut-tutted. "Now, Eleanor, there's nice things, and then there are those Hummels."

The banker cleared his throat. "That had become an... issue. Especially since Molly moved in with Richard. She didn't need an allowance any longer, or at least, not as large a one as she had previously."

Enza sat back, thinking. Richard had been planning to send Molly to a nursing home. That would have pretty much ended the allowance altogether. She looked from the table to the area of the patio outside the French doors, where the door going into the bathroom was. Molly could have made it, Enza thought. Good Lord, the woman had been dancing a reel on the lawn.

She smiled brightly at the banker. "I imagine that was a sore point with Molly? Mr....?"

He stood and reached across the table to shake her hand. "Trulove. Miles Trulove. Personal finance."

She took his hand, half-expecting him to hand her a card.

"And do you believe, Miles?" asked Phyl in a breathless kind of voice.

"Believe what, Ma'am?"

"In true love, of course."

Enza stared at her partner.

Miles blushed. "Well, I personally have found that particular reward rather hard to... earn," he said stiffly.

Phyl reached over and laid her hand on his arm. "It will come, Miles. When you least expect it."

Lloyd, rail-thin and balding, had been standing at the table, knotty hands gripping the back of the empty chair in front of him. "And right you are, missy. True love always finds a way."

Phyl turned to look up at him, and their eyes locked. Lloyd's face softened. Phyl smiled gently.

Enza looked from one to the other. She could almost see it, a current of something running between them, practically lighting up the evening air. Was that sort of thing even possible between total strangers? She waited for a heavenly choir, or at least the gentle strains of a harp, but, no, just two people looking at each other with a certain recognition in their eyes.

"You two want a room?" she asked.

Lloyd cleared his throat and straightened up. "I was just *sayin'*, is all."

"Yes," Phyl gushed.

Jo, next to Enza, rolled her head back. "Please Lord," she muttered, "take me now."

Enza leaned to whisper in Jo's ear. "Are they making goo-goo eyes at each other? There's like, a dead body fifty feet away."

Jo fixed a narrowed eye on her friend. "That didn't stop you from practically tearing the clothes of Mr. Guitar Man," she whispered back.

Enza waved a hand. "Different. We had a connection before there was a body." She sat back, drumming her manicured fingers against the tabletop.

She wanted to pump these little old ladies for more gossip about Molly. She wanted to hear what Molly and Richard were saying to the police. She wanted to see Connor again, just because. She was also hungry, and *really* wanted something to eat.

"I don't suppose," Helen asked, "there's a way we could get some water? I believe in thorough hydration."

Enza bounded up. "Not to worry. I'm sure they won't let us die of thirst out here." One heel sank into the ground, and she pulled the offending shoe off her foot, took off the other one, and marched, barefoot, back into the house.

THE KITCHEN WAS full of men and women in blue. She

looked toward the door to the den and saw Connor. He was on the kitchen side of the half-wall that divided the work-space from the breakfast nook. His back was toward her, and he was leaning his forearms on the wall, watching what was going on in the den. Enza saw the flashing of a light and knew, from years of watching CSI, that pictures were being taken. She spent a few moments appreciating Connor from the back, noticing the excellent fit of his jeans.

She was torn between calling out to him and having him turn to face her, or just continuing to stare at his backside.

She chose to stare, then headed into the dining room.

She moved along the wall, trying to stay out of the line of sight of the living room. She found a spot, right next to the tall and elegant breakfront, and leaned against the wall, listening.

Richard was answering questions in a broken voice. "...No, we just spent the afternoon talking. We had a few vodka tonics, read the Sunday Times, and talked. That's what we usually did on Sundays."

"So, neither of you joined your mother's party?" Enza recognized the voice as Whalen's. "Why didn't you?"

Molly spoke. "This was about all my friends," she said. Her voice sounded strong and impatient. "I told you that already. There was no family invited."

"Except for Ms. Hollowach," Whalen said. Enza thought for a minute. Hollowach? Then realized that was probably Linda, Faith's sister.

"Molly and I had become more than just related by marriage," a composed, low voice said. Linda, Enza reasoned. "We saw each other outside of family gatherings. I considered her a good friend."

Wow, Enza thought. There's sisterly love for you.

Linda continued. "Faith and I did not agree on many

things, but we both held Molly in very high esteem." Enza bit down on her lip to keep from shouting "Liar, liar, pants on fire!"

She heard a shuffling of notes. "It has been suggested," Newberry said, "that Molly McGowan did not share that feeling of esteem for her daughter-in-law. In fact, the word 'hate' was mentioned."

"That's a lie," Richard said hoarsely.

"Now, son," Molly said in a gentle voice. "We need to be honest here. I did not like Faith. I never thought she was right for my son, and I was not shy about letting these feelings be known."

"How long were you married, Mr. McGowan?" Whalen asked.

Richard cleared his throat. "Twenty-eight years."

Someone in the room made a noise, and a voice Enza did not recognize blurted, "And after all that time, you still didn't think she was right for your son?"

There was a general outbreak of rising voices, and Enza leaned forward to try to see into the living room when she felt someone behind her. She froze and turned very slowly. She was staring at a broad chest, covered in a dark shirt, with a small but sexy V at the neck, showing thick, dark hair. She lifted her eyes. Connor closed his eyes, shook his head slightly, grabbed her arm and pulled her back into the kitchen.

"What are you doing here?" he asked in a low voice.

"Helen was thirsty, I was getting water."

"In the dining room?"

"Looking for a glass?"

"Enza, listen—"

"That's what I've been *trying* to do. Can I get back at it?"

"No, you may not. Enza, a woman has been murdered."

"I know. My client."

His expression changed slightly. "I can understand that you feel a certain...responsibility to Faith McGowan, but the truth is, there are very competent detectives here, doing their job, and you should not interfere."

"I was not interfering. I was just standing there."

He tilted his head back and exhaled loudly. "Enza, please. Get a glass of water and go."

"I was thinking more along the lines of a pitcher of water, some glasses, and maybe a little something to munch on? Those ladies out there are pretty old, and who knows how long we're going to be here. Don't want anyone passing out from hunger, do you?" At that moment, her own stomach growled, rather loudly, and Connor broke into a smile.

"The old people are hungry, huh? Okay, let me ask and see what we can do." He went past her, into the living room, and returned moments later with a uniformed officer, a youngish woman, who helped Enza load up a tray with a carafe of water, plastic cups, and the tray of scones Phyl had left behind. As Enza picked up the tray, Whalen walked in, took it from her, and motioned with his head for her to go outside. "I'll take this," he said. "We need to get statements from those folks out there and let them go home."

Enza followed him out. "What about Luxe? When can we go?"

"Well, your two girls can go, but not the three of you who found the body. We need to go over that again." He crossed the lawn and set the tray down in the table with a flourish. "Ladies and gentlemen," he announced. "This officer here will bring you in one at a time to meet with one of our detectives and get a statement, and then you'll be free to go. We'll start with you in the band since none of you had any prior relationship to the victim."

Enza poured water into the cups and passed them around as Phyl uncovered the scones. Detective Whalen escorted one of the band members back to the house. Connor sat, and Enza sat next to him.

"I came with the band," Connor said. "But I'd like to stick around for a while."

Enza arched one perfect eyebrow, "I have my car. I can always give you a lift."

His mouth twitched. "That's very generous of you."

"You know what would be an equally generous thing *you* could do?"

His eyes lit up. "What?"

"Go on in there and listen to all those statements being taken, and then letting me know what was said." His expression changed and Enza sat back, throwing her hands in the air. "What? That way we'll have something to chat about while I drive you home! Swear to God, Connor, is it such a big deal?"

He looked at Jo. "Is she always like this?"

Jo rolled her eyes. "God, yes. Don't encourage her."

Enza nudged his ankle with her foot. "Please? I'd go and sneak in there myself, but if I don't eat soon, it's gonna get ugly."

He looked at her. "I don't know if I want to kiss you or spank you," he said at last.

She reached for a scone and waved it airily. "We can work that all out later. Can you go now? Please?"

He shook his head, got up, and walked back to the house

THE LADIES of Luxe were back in the dining room. There

was no sign of Molly, Richard or Linda. There were no more noises coming from the den. The house was quiet.

"Where did you take the main suspects?" Enza asked as soon as Detective Whalen sat down.

He frowned. "What main suspects?"

She jerked her head in the direction of the living room. "Those guys. Isn't family, and spouses, always the first ones police look at? And is Virginia Crewe on the list?"

Whalen looked at his notes. "Crewe? No. Should she be?"

Enza settled into her chair. "Well. Here's the thing. Virginia was engaged to Richard, Richard met Faith and broke it off, and Virginia never got over it. When I interrupted the two of them, Virginia accused Faith of ruining her life. She, that is, Virginia was crowding Faith, and Faith had to push her back. I had to drag Virginia out of there, and—" She stopped as she suddenly remembered.

"And what, Ms. Biondi?" Whalen asked "What?"

"I heard the door close behind me, and I swear I heard a click," she said slowly. "But I don't *know* if it locked behind me. The door had stayed locked all afternoon, but...maybe... anyone could have gotten in."

Whalen and Newberry exchanged looks. "What time was this?" Newberry asked.

She was exhausted. Phyl was almost asleep in her chair. Even Jo, usually the last to fade, looked like she was about to drop.

"I told you. Five fifteen? Five twenty tops. Weren't you paying attention earlier?" Enza said.

"Good." Whalen took a deep breath. "We just need to go over the afternoon, particularly starting at about five o'clock, when the party was officially over."

He spent another hour with them, picking apart every

word and detail. Newberry sat, taking notes, not saying a word. But Enza saw that while Whalen was watching whoever was speaking at the time, Newberry was watching the other two, observing the reactions to what was being said. Finally, Whalen ran his fingers through his short, gray hair, and closed his notebook. "I trust you ladies will not be leaving the country anytime soon? I case we need to get in touch with you?"

Enza shook her head. "We're booked pretty solid up until July, then we've scheduled a break so we can all get away for a bit." She glanced around. "I don't think anyone's leaving the country."

Jo shook her head. "Vermont."

Phyl sighed. "San Francisco."

Whalen looked at Enza. "And you?"

She shrugged. "I'll be sure to let you know."

"Excellent." He pushed his chair away from the table. "Thank you for your cooperation. If we need anything else, we'll be in touch."

The ladies all stood and walked out to the driveway. Phyl and Jo climbed into the van. Gina and Laurel had taken the other van when they'd left hours earlier. Enza glanced around. Apparently, Connor had gotten a lift from someone else. She was dreaming up little torture scenarios as she walked to her car, then heard him call out. He trotted up to her.

"You were giving me a lift, remember?"

She unlocked the car. "You better believe I remembered. I just didn't know where you were."

He got into the Mercedes beside her. "Just checking something out."

"Yeah? You gonna share? Or do I have to resort to threats of pain and deprivation?"

"Well, I'm not into pain so much, but deprivation sounds kinda kinky."

She grinned as she started the car. "Where am I taking you?"

"Madison."

She put the car in gear and pulled away from the curb. She passed the house, the interior ablaze with light, a long line of cars still in front. "So?"

He had fastened his belt and slouched down in the seat, his long legs stretched out as far as they could go. "Can this seat go back any farther?" he asked.

"No. Besides, if you're too comfortable, you might fall asleep. I think maybe we should talk to keep awake. What did you hear?"

"God, Enza, you don't believe in much foreplay, do you."

"If you're lucky, you may find out the answer to that question. But for now, I want to get to the point."

"Yeah. Well, it looks like there may have been some shady dealing with money."

She nodded. "I know. Richard had his mother on an allowance, but Faith watched every penny. And Molly did not like a short leash. Did that banker guy, Miles Trulove, say anything about the argument he had with Richard?"

He sat up straighter. "What argument?"

"While we were clearing out the kitchen, I came across Richard and Miles arguing, something about being in too deep, Trulove said he was on board, and Richard said that as long as everyone kept their mouth shut..."

"Are you kidding me? Why didn't you say anything about this?"

"Nobody asked! Detective Whalen asked questions and I answered them. And he didn't seem much interested in anything beyond that. In fact, when I offered a theory or two—"

"Enza, there's a difference between offering up a theory and relaying potentially valuable information. Miles Trulove said nothing about an argument."

"I had him pegged for a stinker," Enza muttered. "But that name...I mean, seriously? *Trulove*? Phyl about swooned."

"Anything else you overheard? Or maybe saw? Like somebody wiping blood off their hands or sticking a bloody shirt in a brown paper bag?"

"Why would there be blood? Was there, you know, *spray*?"

He shook his head, looking out the passenger window. "Probably not. The knife used was very long and thin."

"A boning knife?"

He glanced at her. "You know about different kinds of knives?"

"Ones in the kitchen, yes. After all, my partner is a chef, and we've had many long and, if I may say, tedious conversations about what knives to buy and why. Boning knives are used for, well..." She actually didn't know. "Boning things."

He chuckled. "Yes, that's right."

She was at a stoplight, and she impatiently tapped her fingertips on the steering wheel.

"Like traffic lights much?" Connor asked, a teasing note in his voice.

As it changed to green, she hit the gas and took off. "They're my fave."

"Can I ask you a technical question?"

"Sure."

"How the hell do you drive in those heels?"

Enza grinned. "I'm so used to it now, it feels weird when

I'm in flats. The gas pedal is designed for women in heels, by the way. You didn't know that?"

"No, I did not."

"Yeah well, when I started driving, it wasn't like that, and it was a royal pain."

"Oh? And when was *that*?" the teasing note was back.

"When I was twelve," she snapped.

He snorted. "Oh? And where did you live that let you drive when you were twelve?"

"Brooklyn. Listen, are you gonna just shoot the bull here, or talk about something important?"

He sighed. "Is there anything else that you heard or saw that just might be relevant to solving this?"

"This was Molly's going away party. She was heading to a nursing home."

"Knew that."

"She collected Hummels. Antique ones. She got them from dealers."

"Who?"

"Molly. According to Helen, she had them all lined up on her dresser."

He let out a low whistle. "Aren't those valuable?"

"Yep. Where am I going?"

"Right off Main Street, past the center. I have a condo over that way."

"On the same street as the high school?"

"That's right. You know Madison?"

"We used to do a lot of kids parties out here. These parents have money. So, I told you all I know. Your turn."

"Faith McGowan and her sister hadn't spoken in over six months. It seems that Linda, the sister, didn't think good old Molly was being treated fairly, especially when it came to

Molly and money. Linda kind of blurred over a few things there, not evasive, but not exactly straight either."

"I imagine Molly doesn't think anyone treats her fairly."

"Yeah, that's kind of the feeling I got. Kind of...bad-tempered, our Molly."

Enza took a sharp left at around forty miles an hour, causing Connor to hit the inside of the door. "Molly is a bitch."

"I can see we have strong feelings about her," Connor said, straightening himself out.

"I liked Faith," Enza said. "She was a sweet and extremely patient lady, in love with her husband, in a very bad situation. She was probably extremely uncomfortable living with a woman who didn't try to hide her very negative feelings. I gave her a lot of credit. Course, if I had a husband like Richard, I'd probably put up with a whole bunch of crap too."

"Oh? Did you find him attractive?"

She grinned. "Second most attractive man at the party."

Connor laughed and motioned to the row of town-houses that loomed on the right. "Here I am. The second from the end."

She swung to the side of the street and braked sharply, threw the car into Park, and turned to face Connor. "So, I think we should continue this conversation over, say, dinner. I'd invite you to my place one night next week, but I don't cook. I do, however, know some great take-out places. Chinese or Barbecue?"

He reached out his hand and curled his fingers around the back of her neck, drawing her close. He looked steadily into her eyes. She felt her breath quicken. Was he going to kiss her? Because if he was...

"I happen to be an excellent cook. How about Tuesday night? Seven?"

She'd have to wait for a kiss. But only until Tuesday night. "Perfect."

He got out of the car and she watched as he let himself in the front door. Then she gunned the Mercedes down the street toward home.

4

W hen Jo let herself into the Luxe townhouse the next morning, she smelled coffee and headed for the kitchen to find Phyl at the table, laptop open. She glanced around. "Enza?"

Phyl shook her head. "Not yet."

Jo looked over Phyl's shoulder. "French toast recipes? Isn't French toast kind of a standard thing?"

Phyl sighed. "I'm trying to elevate the standard."

Of course, Jo thought. Phyl would try to elevate peanut butter and jelly.

She heard footsteps on the stairs as Enza came into the kitchen, hair mussed up on one side, feet bare, wearing silky jammy pants and a sleeveless top, lacy and low-cut.

"How are you even awake?" Enza grumbled, heading for the Keurig.

Jo eyed her with suspicion. "Did you sleep with Connor last night?" she asked. She knew that Enza enjoyed the company of men and was not at all shy in talking about it.

"No, I did not," Enza said hotly. "Please, I just met him."

"Sorry," Jo said, surprised by Enza's defensiveness. "It's

just that, you know, you look like...well...like you had company." Jo tended to sleep in T-shirts and sweatpants, company or not.

Enza poured sugar in her coffee. "Don't be bitchy. I'll get dressed in a few minutes. I just came down to see what you two were up to." She sipped. "You realize, of course, that we were never paid last night."

Jo had not realized. Her shoulders slumped. Luxe usually received their last payment, the last third, at the end of the event. But last night..."God, you're right."

"You're the business end of this, Enza," Phyl said. "I'm sure you'll find a kind and tactful way to get the grieving widower to write us a check."

Enza sighed. "Right. What are you up to?"

Phyl was squinting at her laptop. "Trying to put together a menu for that breakfast meeting. The one for the hospital? I was thinking a French toast thing that I could pre-bake in the oven, and maybe an omelet station?"

Enza sipped. "Sounds good. Jo? What's goin' on?"

Jo pulled out her phone and re-checked her texts. "We have to be back at the McGowan house today at two. The rental guys are coming to get the tables and chairs. I checked with the police. There are still people on the scene, I think, but we're okay to clear out the rest of our stuff. The rental guys are being very good about this. Usually, they're a pain in the butt about everything, but this time..."

Enza shrugged. "Can we get delay-by-death discount?"

Jo snorted. "They're not being *that* good."

"I'll come with you," Enza said. "I want another look around." She sat down at the table and cradled her mug in her hands. "Who did you speak to when you called the police?" she asked Jo.

"Does it matter? Some detective."

"Whalen or Newberry?"

"Whalen. He's very polite." Jo narrowed her eyes at her friend. "Why?"

"Because our client was murdered, we were right there, and I want to make sure they find the killer, that's why."

Phyl closed her laptop. "I keep remembering what happened last time, Enza. You ended up with stitches in your foot and that crazy man could have killed you."

"But he didn't," Enza countered. "My ninja partner rescued us at the last minute."

Luxe had catered a birthday party at the Lake Abrams Club House, and a guest ended up with her scarf tied too tightly around her neck. Enza had joined forces with Ellie Rocca, who had hired them, and the two women tracked down the killer in his own basement. It could have gone quite wrong for the two of them, but the cavalry, in the form of Jo and Homicide Detective Sam Kinali, had arrived just in the nick of time. Jo had acted instinctively in defending her friend, calling on her years of self-defense training, and had taken down the bad guy in a brief series of moves that flattened him completely. She still vividly remembered how terrified she'd been.

Jo leaned over and pointed her finger at Enza. "Do not think," she said distinctly, "that I am going to be on rescue duty if you decide to stick your nose in where it doesn't belong *again*. That little episode was a one-shot deal."

Enza rolled her eyes. "Did I tell you, Phyl? How she flattened that old man with a couple of fast ju-jitsu moves?"

Phyl sighed. "Many times. And I appreciate that Faith McGowan was a lovely woman, and what happened to her was truly horrific. But we plan parties, Enza. We do not solve murders."

"I know that." Enza stood. "I just want to make sure the

police are on the right track. I'm going to shower and dress. I'll be back down in a few."

She was almost out of the kitchen when Phyl's voice stopped her.

"Connor Ives called this morning. On the office line."

Enza made an about-face and went back to the dining room. "And you waited to tell me because?"

Jo grinned at the expression of Enza's face. "So, his calling is significant? Where did you two go last night?"

"Nowhere. I took him home. What did he say?"

Phyl peeled a Post-it from a stack of papers. "He just wanted you to have his number. Wasn't that sweet of him, Jo?"

Was Enza *blushing*? Oh, Jo thought, this could get very interesting. "Yes. *Very* sweet. Such a gentleman. And did you notice, Phyl? That marvelous butt of his?"

"Why, Jo," Phyl gushed, "as a matter of fact, I *did* notice. Enza, what did *you* think of his butt?"

Enza snatched the Post-it out of Jo's hand and marched out, with, Jo thought, considerable dignity for a woman in lace pajamas.

ENZA CALLED the number on the card that Detective Whalen had given her, leaving a brief message that she was going to be at the McGowan house after two that afternoon, and he should probably meet her there, as she had overheard something the night before that may be relevant to the case. Then she called the municipal building in Basking Ridge and asked how she could get a permit for a horse-drawn carriage to trot down Main Street for her client's wedding. The person in the other end of the line was clueless, took Enza's number, and promised to call back.

She then spent ten minutes staring at Connor Ives phone number, trying to think of a reason, any reason in the world, to call a special investigator for the FBI on his personal cell phone in the middle of the day. There was none to be found.

She called him anyway but went straight to voicemail. "Hey, Connor, this is Enza. I know you're probably working on something really important, but I just wanted you to know that I'm going to tell Detective Whalen about the fight. You know, the Miles and Richard fight? That's all. Just wanted you to know that. And, oh, yeah, I'm looking forward to tomorrow. Should I bring something? Wine? I'll bring wine. Just call me back and let me know if I should bring red or white. No, never mind, you're busy, I'll bring both. And maybe a dessert wine. Okay, that's all. Really. Bye."

She clicked off the phone, closed her eyes, thought about all she had just said, and banged her head, slowly, repeatedly, against the top of her desk.

Jo heard the slow thumping and stuck her head in the office door. "The Basking Ridge bride?" she asked, concerned.

Enza looked up. "No. The hot guitar guy. I just left a five-minute voicemail message when three sentences would have done the job. I feel twelve all over again." She dropped her head again.

"Oh, my," Jo said, grinning. "He did get to you, didn't he?"

"His day job is with the FBI, did I tell you?"

"No, you didn't. That's interesting. What else do you know about him?"

"He lives in Madison and he has very sexy forearms."

"Oh? Well, okay, I was thinking more along the lines of his, you know, being married..."

Enza lifted her head off the desk, swearing. She hit redial and again went to voicemail. "By the way, if you're married, please tell me right away so I can drink all that wine by myself." She clicked off the phone.

Jo's jaw dropped. "Oh, my, God, Enza, did you really just leave a message like that?"

Enza looked smug. "You heard me, right? If he is married, I'll be getting drunk tomorrow night. Want to join me?"

"No, thanks."

"If we can't get a permit for six palominos to drive down Main Street in Basking Ridge, do we have a Plan B?"

"Balloon ride?"

"Too many trees around the church."

"Antique Rolls Royce?"

Enza snorted. "That was my first suggestion. She said it was too common."

Jo let out a low whistle. "Half-naked body-builders pulling rickshaws?"

Enza frowned. "Let me write that one down, just in case."

"I hate brides."

Enza nodded. "Me too."

THERE WAS yellow tape across the driveway of the McGowan house. Enza parked down the street and she and Jo walked up to the front door and rang the bell.

Detective Whalen answered. "Ms. Biondi. Ms. Collins. A pleasure to see you again. I think."

Enza waved her hand in the direction of the driveway.

"Can you get someone to take down the tape? My guys will be here any minute, and it would help if they could get closer to the back yard."

Whalen looked at Enza, then switched his stare to Jo, then back to Enza. "Yeah, I'll do that, but Ms. Biondi? If you could step inside? I believe you have something to tell me?"

Enza sighed and followed Whalen inside, through the living room, and into the all-too-familiar dining room. A uniformed officer stepped up at Whalen's word and went outside to remove the tape. Jo followed with a backward glance.

Enza settled herself in a chair. "So, Detective, how's the investigation going so far?"

He sat and stared at her. "Why, it's going fine. Nice of you to ask."

She leaned a bit toward him. "Have you questioned Virginia Crewe?"

He sighed. "I hope you understand that it is not customary to discuss and ongoing investigation with anyone *outside* of the investigation."

She shrugged. "It doesn't hurt to ask. But before we get going here, have you known Connor a long time?"

He blinked, then burst out laughing. "Are you kidding me? Did you lure me here just to ask about Connor?"

She drummed her nails on the tabletop. "I did not lure you here. I did overhear something that might be significant. But while we're chatting..?"

He was still chuckling as he shook his head and took out his notebook.

Detective Newberry came in from the kitchen and looked from Whalen to Enza. "Something funny?"

"Yeah," Whalen said. "Looks like Ms. Biondi here has the hots for Ives."

"I do not," she said coldly, "Get the hots for any man."

Whalen cleared his throat. "Sure. Now, what about this significant thing you may have overheard?"

She told him everything she could remember. He and Newberry listened, Newberry took notes, and when she was done, the two men exchanged glances.

"This was Miles Trulove?" Whalen asked. "You're sure?"

She nodded. "Yes, I'm sure, because he was one of the guests that was still here after the body was found. We spent some real quality time out back, waiting to give our statements."

"Did you ask him about the argument?" Newberry asked.

She rolled her eyes. "Do I look like an idiot? Of course not. I didn't want him to know what I'd heard. What if it was, you know, a clue?"

"And yet," Whalen said, his voice getting sharp, "you failed to mention it to us when we questioned you."

"Please," Enza said, throwing up her hands. "Don't even start with that. You asked me very specific questions, and I answered them truthfully. If you had bothered to ask if I had anything else of interest to add, well, maybe..."

Whalen shook his head. "You're a piece work, you know that? Well, whatever. Thank you for this. It is helpful." He paused, then leaned forward. "Is there anything else of interest you'd like to add, Ms. Biondi?"

Enza frowned, looked thoughtful, and even scratched her head with a bright red fingernail. "Can't think of a thing," she said at last.

Whalen stood up, as did Enza. He walked her to the French doors and nodded as she walked out.

Enza looked out into the backyard and saw Jo with Gary from the rental company. Jo looked like she had everything under control, so Enza turned around and went back into the house.

Whalen and Newberry were nowhere to be seen. She moved quietly through the kitchen and dining room, then the living room and past the front door. There was more crime scene tape there, she noted, as she went down the hallway, passed the graceful, sweeping staircase, and farther down the hall.

There was an obvious door to the garage, and another, door, six-paneled and painted white. Molly's room, she thought.

She pushed open the door cautiously.

It was a smallish but pleasant room, probably originally meant for the maid. There was a queen-sized bed with a colorful, obviously hand-made quilt, antique cherry furniture, and a comfortable armchair by the double windows. She took another step in. A tall bookcase was next to the bed, and a small, flat-screen television sat on a stand. The dresser was full of framed pictures, and as Enza looked, she recognized some of the faces as those she saw at the party. There were several of Molly and Richard through the years, but none of Faith.

She opened the double door to the closet and riffled through the clothes hanging there. Plain cotton dresses and blouses, simple cardigans, and several pair of slippers and loafers lined up very neatly. As she turned, a flash of color caught her eye. There, on the floor of the closet was a bright purple scarf.

Enza stopped and picked it up. Virginia Crewe's scarf. In Molly's closet. What on earth was it doing there?

Enza slipped the scarf into her purse, closed the closet and glanced over at the bookshelf. Lots of paperback romance novels, and a leather-bound complete works of Shakespeare.

She slipped out of the bedroom, hurried down the hall, and was out into the backyard again, just as Jo was coming up.

"Where were you?" Jo asked. "Are you done in there with the police?"

Enza nodded, frowning. There was something wrong, but what?

"Enza?" Jo said sharply. "What?"

Enza looked at her friend and partner, her mind going off into several different directions. "You remember last night when we were waiting and Molly's friends were talking?"

Jo nodded impatiently. "Of course. So what?"

"Where are the Hummels?"

Jo frowned. "What are you talking about?"

Enza shook her head. "Never mind. Are we almost done here?"

Jo nodded, and Enza followed her down the driveway. But the thought was there, a persistent drip.

Where were all those Hummel figurines that Molly loved so much?

PHYL WAS BAKING. Baking was one of her favorite things in the world to do, and when she was baking for someone special, well...

She held out the still-warm butter cookie. "Take a taste?" she asked.

Lloyd opened his mouth. Phyl delicately dropped the cookie on his tongue and smiled as he chewed, his eyes closed, his face radiating obvious delight.

Phyl usually didn't invite men to keep her company at work. In fact, she had never before invited a man to the office, not in her two years at Luxe. But then, she'd never met a man quite like Lloyd. He had asked her for her phone number, and when she'd finally left the McGowan house the night before, she found a message from him on her cell phone. Would she care for a cup of coffee? She met him at a nearby diner and the two had talked long into the night. When Lloyd knocked on the door of the Luxe townhouse in the early afternoon, saying he wanted to see her, she didn't hesitate to ask him in.

She heard Enza's heels on the wooden floor and watched as her partner came through the door.

"Lloyd?" Enza asked, blinking.

"Why, yes," Phyl said brightly. "He was the leader of the band at the party last night, remember? And he played the bouzouki. Lloyd, of course, you remember my partner, Enza Biondi?"

Lloyd cast one look of longing at Phyl and her cookie, then smiled and bowed at Enza. "Of course. A real pleasure to see you again, my dear. And under much better circumstances. I hope you don't mind my dropping in on Phyllis here at her place of employment, but I didn't know how else to find her."

Enza frowned. "No, I don't mind. As long as Phyl doesn't."

Phyl sighed with pleasure. "No," she said. "Not at all." She placed another cookie between his lips. He bit down, closed his eyes, and chewed slowly.

"Just like my mother used to make," he said.

Phyl beamed.

"Ah..." Enza stepped back just a little.

Lloyd swallowed and turned back to Enza. "And how are you and my nephew getting on?"

Enza looked even more confused. "Nephew? What nephew?"

"Connor," Lloyd said. "Not my real nephew of course. His mother and my sister were the best of friends, you see, and when Connor's father dropped out of the picture, I sort of stepped in. As a father figure, you understand."

No," she said bluntly. "I don't understand."

Lloyd put his elbow on the counter and appeared to settle in. "Well, now, Connor's father was a very important figure in what can best be described as a neighborhood social organization. This was up in Boston, you see. I myself was also a member of said organization, although I was way down in the line of succession. Now, John Ives was a well-respected man, feared and admired in the community, but he got a bit sloppy there in the sixties and allowed himself to be, how can I put this? Eliminated by a rival organization. That left his poor wife and only son without, shall we say, any visible means of support, John not being the sort of man to trust banks and stocks and the like."

Enza drew up a stool to sit on. "Connor's father was a gangster?" Phyl pushed a few cookies in Enza's direction and Enza absently took one. "Who got knocked off?"

"Indeed," Lloyd said.

"What happened?" Enza asked, chewing her cookie.

"Well, Connor's mother, Elaine, moved away from Boston and down here to this lovely area, where she started a new life for herself and her son. My sister, whose husband had, shall we say, followed in John's footsteps, came down here as well."

"And you?" Enza asked. "You're also a crook?"

Lloyd made a visible effort to think about that one. "Not

76

exactly. That is, not anymore. I consider myself a full-time musician, you see."

"But before that," Enza prompted. "You were a crook?"

Enza," Phyl protested softly. "I don't think that's our business." Although Lloyd had explained, in exacting detail, his rather checkered past, Phyl was not about to hold it against the man. After all, he had awakened something in her, something she had thought dead years ago, and she was not about to let a little thing like a felony record cloud her feelings toward him.

Lloyd waved a hand. "Now, Phyllis, darlin', of course it's her business. After all, this is her establishment as well, and she is naturally curious about anyone who is spending time here, and she has every right to ask questions."

Enza, now sitting down, almost fell off the stool at the words *spending time.*

Lloyd cleared his throat and smoothed a few pale strands of hair across the top of his head. "I, myself, did spend a few very trying years of my youth behind bars, as a matter of fact. But I saw the error of my ways and have tried to be an upstanding citizen since my release back into the general population. In fact, I completely removed myself from any possible temptation to step back, as they say, into the fold and moved down this way. To live with my sister, you see, in as honest a way possible."

"And when was that?" Enza asked.

"Thirty-three years ago," Lloyd answered promptly.

Enza turned from staring at Lloyd to stare at Phyl. "Did you know this?"

Phyl sighed. "Of course, Enza. Lloyd and I have no secrets."

Enza blinked. "No secrets? You just met him yesterday! You've only spent, what, three or four hours with him?"

Phyl pursed her lips, thinking. "We spent quite a bit of time together. Last night. We talked and talked until quite late."

Lloyd beamed and patted Phyl's hand. "Was that only last night? It seems like I've known you forever."

Phyl nodded. "I feel the same way." She looked into his pale blue eyes and felt a tug of something deep in her soul.

Enza slid down off the stool. "I think I need a drink. What time is it anyway? Too early for a bit of something?"

Lloyd straightened. "It's never too early for a bit of something, Enza. What have you got?"

Enza crossed the kitchen, opened up a bottom cabinet and pulled out a bottle. "Jack Daniels?"

Lloyd grimaced. "Well, I suppose, in a pinch."

Enza found the juice glasses and poured a few fingers worth of Jack Daniels in two of them. Phyl shook her head when Enza motioned to pour in the third. Phyl didn't like strong drink and knew that Enza normally didn't either. It seemed that her friend and partner was a bit shaken by all that Lloyd had said.

"So, let me get this straight," she said. "Connor's father was an Irish mob guy in Boston who got killed by another mob, you were also a member of said mob, and when you got out of prison, you followed your sister down here, and have been acting as Connor's uncle while playing in an Irish band for thirty years?"

He pushed his empty glass toward Enza. "Yes, that's it."

"And Connor went from being a gangster's son to an FBI investigator?"

"Well," Lloyd made a face. "It would not have been my choice, you understand, but he seems to have made quite a go of it." He pushed his glass a little closer to the bottle and raised an eyebrow.

"Sorry," Enza mumbled as she poured him a bit more. Then she looked at Phyl. "And you know this already because he took you back to his place last night? Where you stayed?"

Phyl smiled dreamily. "No. We met at a diner. We thought we were going to just have a cup of coffee, but we ended up sitting there half the night."

Enza put up both hands, palms out, as to stop an oncoming train. "Of course. And why not? I get it. I think." She drummed her nails against the countertop. "I don't suppose that during your thirty-some years of honest living, you, maybe, crossed a few lines?"

Lloyd held out his glass and looked thoughtful. "Possibly. Why?"

She poured him more Jack Daniels. "Well, I was thinking more about getting some inside information from the police."

Lloyd beamed. "My dear, I have contacts everywhere. On both sides of the law. Being a musician makes for very strange bedfellows, indeed."

"Indeed," Enza repeated. "You didn't know any of the detectives that were at the McGowan's?"

He shook his head. "No, that's not my preferred neighborhood. But that doesn't mean I can't get a bit of information if you be needing it."

Enza nodded. "Yes, I be needing it. Can you find out about Molly's Hummel figurines? She was supposed to have had a collection of them, and they would have been worth a lot of money. Where did they go? Where did the money go?"

He downed his drink and smacked his lips. "I can make a few calls. Give me a day or two. And now, Phyllis, my love, we were going to get a bite of something? You'll have to drive, I'm afraid. I never drink and drive."

Phyl reached over and gave him a quick kiss on the cheek. "How responsible of you. Of course. Let me get my purse."

She scurried off, leaving Enza and Lloyd alone. Her heart was singing. She was closing in on sixty and had thought her life over when she met Jo and Enza. They had welcomed her and her talent into their business and their hearts, giving her back a career she loved. And now, to meet a man this late in her life was nothing short of a miracle.

She hurried back to the kitchen, pausing outside the doorway. She didn't mean to listen in, but...

"I feel I should warn you," Enza said. "She's not a very good driver."

Phyl imagined Lloyd shrugging. "I knew there had to be a flaw somewhere."

Enza paused. "If you break her heart," she said, her voice low and even, "I will hunt you down and hurt you."

Lloyd sighed loudly. "I don't doubt that for a minute. But, believe it or not, when I look at that magnificent woman, I see all of my dreams, those broken and those still blooming in my soul, coming together in one joyous, loving whole." He sighed again. "I love her. I'll take an arrow through my heart for her."

Phyl stepped through the doorway. "Ready, Lloyd?"

He grinned and winked at Enza. "And she cooks." He straightened and practically did a jig down the hallway, the top of his head barely meeting Phyl's shoulder.

Phyl turned at the front door, beaming like a schoolgirl, waved to Enza and shut the door.

IT WAS LATE when Connor finally called, and Enza stared at her phone for three whole rings.

Should she answer right away? She didn't want to appear too eager. Should she just let it go to voicemail? If he was calling to tell her he was, indeed, married, it would be better to just stare at the phone, perhaps scream a bit, and maybe throw the offending instrument against the wall. Of course, if she did answer, she would have the extreme satisfaction of telling him what a rotten and thoroughly despicable human being he was.

What if he wasn't married at all, and was calling just to hear her voice? Or suggest they not wait until tomorrow, and that she should come to Madison immediately, where he would be waiting, candles lit...

She shook her head as visions of Phyl and Lloyd swam before her eyes.

"Hello?"

"It's Connor. I hope it's not too late, but I was stuck on something at work. How did your meeting go today with my friend Detective Whalen?"

Friend? Really? And had that friend mentioned how *she* mentioned... "I'm not sure he likes me very much," she said. "I may have aggravated him. A bit."

Connor laughed, a deep and throaty sound. "He likes the challenge, I think."

"*Me* a challenge? He was the one not very forthcoming with information," she said.

"And what information did you think he was going to share with you?"

She sighed. "I don't know. There I was, being all-helpful, telling him everything I knew, and he didn't throw me a scrap. I mean...do you know about Molly's figurines?"

"Pardon?"

"Molly McGovern. She collected antique Hummel figurines, which are rare and expensive. Faith had cut back her allowance, and I guess Molly couldn't buy them anymore. But when I looked in her room, I couldn't find a one. What happened to them?"

"Wait...how do you know this and...what? You looked in her *room*?"

"Well, yes. No one told me I couldn't. And there wasn't any yellow tape across the doorway. Helen said she kept them on her dresser, but they weren't there. Did she sell them? And if she did, why?"

She heard a long, drawn-out breath. "Enza, was this before or after your conversation with Detective Whalen?"

"After."

"And I don't suppose you, you know, tried to find him and tell him any of this?"

"Well." She was lying in bed and sank deeper into the pillows. She had muted the television and stared at the silent screen. "No."

She heard him sigh again. "Enza, this is not my investigation. I have nothing to tell you about Molly's Hummels or anything else. But, once again, an important fact has been withheld from the police. By you."

"So, I guess I'll give him another call. But maybe I should wait for Lloyd."

"Lloyd? You mean, Lloyd Turner?"

"Is that his last name? Your uncle Lloyd. It looks as though he and my business partner have found profound love and deep understanding, and I think they're planning happily ever after. Anyway, he was here at the office when I got back, and we...chatted, and he said he'd ask one of his contacts about what's going on in the case."

There was a brief but heartfelt string of expletives on the line. Enza winced.

"Lloyd is not a person to be putting any kind of faith in," Connor said at last. "He's…"

"I know what he is. He told me all about it." She didn't say that Lloyd also told her all about Connor's father. She just rearranged her pillows and waited.

"Tell me again why you're so interested in all this?"

"Because I liked Faith," Enza explained. "And she was my client. And I'm not sure the police are on the right track. It's about justice, Connor, that's all."

"Hmmm…well, maybe if the police knew everything you knew, they would be on the right track. Whalen is right."

Enza rolled her eyes. "About me? Being a challenge? Can we change the subject?"

"Sure…" His voice dropped to a low purr. "But I think you are. Challenging. I think that maybe it's going to take me a while to peel off all the layers."

She closed her eyes and felt a little shiver go down her throat. All the way down. Talk about a change of subject. "Why, Connor, I do believe you're trying to seduce me over the phone."

"Is it working? I'm thinking if I get a head start, I may not have to cook anything at all tomorrow."

She shook her head. If he was going to go there… "What are you wearing?"

There was a pause. "Just jeans. And I do mean, *just* jeans. And you?"

She looked down at her curvy body, in silky black sleep shorts and a pale gray, lace top. She stretched out her leg and wriggled her red toes. "Sweatpants. My brother's old football jersey. Oh, and I've got on a facial mask. Green clay. Want to know what I'm doing to my hair?"

"What?"

She grinned. "Listen, Connor, you better stick to plan A and cook me something amazing, and then you'd better top off the evening with brilliant conversation and dazzling charm. And if you think you're going to be peeling off anything, you'd better think again. You may be a tall, sexy thing, but I've shut down better men than you, and I didn't even feel bad about it."

Silence, then a full-throated laugh. "Enza, you got me. OK, dinner it is. Are you a steak girl?"

"Yes. Medium. With mushrooms and lots of sautéed onions."

"Then you'd better bring red wine."

"Perfect. Now I know just the right one to bring. And I'll pick up something from the bakery, just a bit of a sweet."

"And I'm not married."

"Damn good thing, too."

"So, I'll see you tomorrow night."

"Yep. I'll be the one wearing the chastity belt."

He laughed again and hung up. Enza stared at the phone, then burst into a fit of giggles and punched the pillow beside her, while the voice in her head kept squealing, yes, yes, yes.

THE NEXT MORNING when Jo came to work, Enza was at her desk, brow wrinkled in concentration, and a look on her face that Jo recognized.

"Why are you looking like that?" she asked.

Enza lifted her eyes from the computer screen. "Like what?"

Jo came in slowly and sank into one of the chairs facing Enza's desk. "Like you're about to do something you shouldn't."

"You're being silly, Jo."

84

"I'm not being silly. What are you doing?"

"Looking over the guest list of the McGowan party."

"Why?"

"Why not? Did Gary send us an invoice yet? For the McGowan party?"

"Yes, of course. It was sitting in my inbox yesterday by five. He only charged us the hourly rate for Sunday afternoon, thank God. What?"

"Nothing," Enza said lightly.

"No, not nothing. I know you, Enza Biondi. I can see your brain churning."

"There's an obituary for Faith this morning, but no scheduled service yet."

Jo shrugged. "They probably have to wait until her body is released."

"Hmmm...right. Did you know that yesterday I found Phyllis in the kitchen, feeding butter cookies to Lloyd? The Irish bouzouki player?"

Jo sat back, mouth open. "Phyllis?"

"Yep. Our Phyllis. In all the time we've known her, she's never mentioned a man in her life, except her snake of an ex-husband, and that was years ago. I kinda thought she had written off that part of her life."

Jo let out a long, low whistle. "Phyllis? Well, good for her. It's good to know that it's never too late."

"Well, you could have knocked me over with a feather. They were like sixteen-year-olds here yesterday." Enza closed her laptop. "He told me he was in love."

"Ah, Enza," Jo sighed. 'That's so sweet."

Jo herself had been rather unlucky in love. She'd been engaged to her high school sweetheart all through college and had repeatedly put off their wedding for years while she built her career. It was only after a brief and quite unexpected encounter with her manager's sister at an office Christmas party that she realized the real reason she didn't want to marry him, and she'd been gun-shy of both sexes since.

"Oh, sure. Sweet. He filled me in on his wayward youth as a career criminal in Boston. However, he saw the error of his ways after a particularly difficult incarceration and has been a career musician for the past thirty years."

Jo made a face. "Well, that's good, right?"

"That's very good since his past experiences have given him some very useful connections. He's going to try to find out all he can about the McGowan case."

Jo had been afraid of this all along. She smacked her palm on the top of Enza's desk. "I knew it! You're not going to let that go, are you?"

"I can't. Who would have wanted to kill that woman? Besides Molly, that is. Not that I don't think Molly isn't perfectly capable of murder, especially if she found out that Faith was shipping her off to a nursing home, but...I don't know. I don't think it's all that cut and dry."

Jo didn't want to say or do anything to encourage Enza, but..."It's not, because it wasn't just Faith, was it? I mean I'm sure Faith would never arrange something like that without Richard's endorsement."

"True." Enza drummed her nails against her desktop. "Virginia Crewe probably had enough pent-up rage to do it, I bet, but Faith could have pushed her over with her little finger."

"Faith was sitting in a chair, her back to the door," Jo mused, visualizing the den as she saw it that afternoon. "Anyone could have sneaked up behind her..." She frowned. "What was the angle of the knife, I wonder? Because to stab her from behind while she was sitting down...that would take a pretty tall person, don't you think? And it would still be awkward. Or was she stabbed from the front?"

Enza nodded. "Good questions. And I don't have any answers. *And* I don't have any way to get the answers. Yet. Then there's the money angle. Always follow the money, Jo."

"Who are you, Jessica Fletcher?"

Enza pushed herself away from her desk. "Don't be silly." She spread her arms, revealing her shapely body, today encased in a Kelly-Green pencil skirt, a white sleeveless tank top that looked like a second skin, and a flowered cardigan of white, bright blue and more Kelly-green blossoms. "Do I look like a little old lady crime fighter?"

"No, but like I said, I can see your brain churning."

Enza waved a hand. "Jo, you worry too much. I have to see a man about six palominos."

"Will you be back for lunch? We need to go over the Froelich dinner."

"No, sorry. Hot lunch date."

Jo raised an eyebrow. "With Connor Ives?"

Enza shook her head. "No. A few of the ladies from the McGowan party."

Jo followed her out and down the hallway. "You're taking Molly McGowan's guests out to lunch?"

"Sure," Enza said. "How else am I going to get them to talk to me about Molly? But I should be back by two. We'll talk then."

Enza scooped up her bag and left Jo listening to the sound of spiked heels clattering on the old, hardwood floor.

5

Enza met MaryBeth Riley in a small pub in Summit, huddled in a corner booth with Helen of the thorough hydration conversation the night of the party. They were both reading the menu with fierce concentration. Enza slid in opposite them and carefully rearranged her face to hide both her excitement and curiosity.

"Ladies, thank you so much for meeting me." She glanced around. "Eleanor couldn't join us?"

Helen sniffed. "Eleanor is indisposed. "

"Oh?" Enza said, concerned.

MaryBeth made a face. "Which means she's still trying to get over her Sunday hangover. Eleanor can't hold her whiskey like she used to."

Helen clucked. "No, poor dear. But then, none of us can."

"Ah. And how is dear Molly?" she asked, lowering her voice to an appropriate hush.

MaryBeth shook her head. "Well, of course she's devastated."

"No, she's not," Helen snapped. "She feels badly, of course, but for Richard and what he's going through. She never had a drop of warmth toward Faith when she was alive, and she certainly isn't going to play for sympathy now." The waitress appeared, and Helen looked sharply at Enza. "You buyin'?"

Enza nodded.

"Good," Helen said. "In that case, I'll have the Rueben, extra fries, and an Irish coffee. You can bring the drink now, thank you very much. And water. A big glass as soon as you can."

MaryBeth closed her menu. "The same."

Enza grabbed a menu and took a quick look. "The same for me too, I guess. But no Irish coffee. Just, you know, regular."

The waitress gathered the menus and left. Helen folded her hands together and sniffed. "They're not allowed back in the house, you know," she whispered. "It's still a crime scene. Lord knows when they can get back in."

Enza waited until the waitress arranged the water glasses and Irish coffees on the table before leaning forward. "Where are they staying?" She asked, thinking, why are we whispering?

"With Linda," Helen said, taking a long sip of her water. "She has graciously opened her home."

"Ah." Enza nodded and sat back. "I gathered that Linda and Molly got along very well."

MaryBeth sighed. "Yes, they did. Poor Faith, she never had a chance with Molly. No woman would ever have been good enough, not after Virginia. And it's a shame, because Faith and Linda are very much alike. I think if Molly hadn't been so stubborn, she and Faith would have been great friends. As it was, Linda almost...took Faith's place."

Helen made a rude, slurping noise as she sipped her Irish coffee. "Linda is an opportunistic bitch who never got over Faith getting all that money and the good-looking husband to boot."

Enza tried to keep both eyebrows from popping off the top of her head. She didn't really think the ladies would be so candid. "There was bad blood?"

MaryBeth looked disapprovingly at Helen and clucked. "Bad blood is putting it mildly. God knows, Faith tried, but Molly was a hard nut to crack."

Helen slurped again.

"Yet, Faith let her live in her home," Enza said.

MaryBeth sniffed. "She had her own place for years, Molly did. Very nice little apartment, right on the bus line. Richard and Faith paid the rent and gave her an allowance. But last year she fell and broke her hip, and she was never the same after that, poor soul. She couldn't live alone anymore. There were a few live-in ladies, and to be honest, they seemed just fine to me but..." She sniffed again. "They weren't good enough for Molly. Faith had no choice, did she? Where else was she going to live?"

The waitress arrived with their plates. Enza stared at her plate, heaped with corned beef and melting cheese, with slick pools of dressing forming around the edges of the toasted bread. She glanced over at her guests, who were happily attacking their own sandwiches with knife and fork. Enza sighed. After eating this, she would feel like a blimp going over to Connor's and, even worse, might not be able to eat any of his steak dinner.

"Tell me more about Virginia," she said.

Helen let out a breath. "Poor Virginia. Always a wallflower. Tiny, insignificant thing. Molly introduced her to Richard. Well, it made sense. If Richard had married a woman like Virginia, then Molly would never have to cede an inch of influence in Richard's life."

MaryBeth wrestled with cutting her sandwich. "Then, Faith came along. Pushed Virginia right out. Molly was furious, of course. She'd never be able to control her son with Faith in the picture. But Richard fell in love, and poor Virginia, well, she never got over it. She still lives in the same apartment she grew up in. She never left the old neighborhood, never married…sad, really."

"And what old neighborhood was that?" Enza asked.

"Bayonne." Helen snorted. "If Virginia had a spine she could have made a life for herself instead of spending the best years of her life pining away in a two bedroom walkup." She pointed her fork at Enza. "Molly visited her regular. That didn't help."

Enza rearranged her fries. "That's all very interesting. Molly invited Virginia to, what? Hurt Faith?"

MaryBeth nodded. "Molly liked Virginia. I think she always hoped Richard would see the error of his ways and dump Faith. She was a little bit delusional when it came to Richard and Faith. She always talked like they were on the brink of divorce."

"Maybe they were?" Enza suggested.

Helen shook her head. "I doubt it. You had to know Molly. She *really* didn't like Faith."

Enza chewed a bit of corned beef. "I wanted to ask you ladies about Molly's collection of Hummels. They sounded beautiful, but, well, wasn't she worried about them being stolen? Wouldn't she have wanted them in a safe place?"

Helen, her cheeks stuffed, chipmunk-style, shook her head, swallowed, and took another gulp of her Irish coffee. "No, Molly was proud of her things, she was. She never had much, but she made sure you got a look at the good stuff."

"So," Enza continued, shaving a bit of corned beef and pushing it from one side of the plate to the other, "Molly had all those Hummels just out for the world to see? Even after she moved in with Richard?"

MaryBeth was chewing a bit slower than Helen and looked thoughtful. "Now that you mention it, I didn't see them in her room over at Richard's place, did you Helen?"

Helen shrugged, and happily drank down more Irish coffee. "I was never in her room at Richard's. We always stayed in the kitchen there, or, when she was feeling grand, in the living room. She liked all that beautiful furniture, Molly did. As much as she complained about missing her own place, she liked Richard's things."

"Richard's and Faith's," Enza reminded her.

Helen shook her head. "Molly never acknowledged that anything in that house belonged to Faith. She didn't like to think about Faith having all the money."

Enza froze, a French fry halfway into the ketchup. "Faith had all the money?"

Helen dropped her voice again. "Richard had a good job, of course. And he did very well for himself. Very well indeed. But Faith was stinkin' rich." She nodded. "Inherited a bundle from her godmother, I understand. We're talking millions."

Enza lowered her French fry. "Millions?"

Helen sighed happily. "I'm pretty sure."

MaryBeth clucked. "Helen, you're going to give Enza the wrong idea about Molly."

"What wrong idea? The woman is buying me lunch! She deserves the truth." Helen pointed her fork at Enza. "Molly hated Faith. Hated her having the money. Hated her having control of the money. Hated the fact that Richard alone could not have kept her in that nice apartment all those years. And she especially hated the fact that Faith at any moment could put her in a nursing home." She signaled the waitress and pointed to her Irish coffee. "Can I get another?" she asked Enza.

Enza nodded. "As many as you want. Did you tell this to the police?"

Helen snorted. "Whatever for?"

"Well," Enza reasoned, "that kind of sounds like motive to me."

Both Helen and MaryBeth froze.

"Motive?" MaryBeth whispered.

Enza looked from one stunned face to the other. "You mean it never occurred to you that Molly, with all that hatred inside her, might have killed Faith?"

"Why, never," Helen gasped, obviously scandalized by the very idea. "Molly is a very devout and good woman. Whatever feelings she may have had in her heart, she never would have done anything so evil."

"That's right," MaryBeth said. "Why, she never missed Sunday mass at St. Timothy's, she was such a saintly person," she added, looking sideways at Helen with raised eyebrows. "And she would have cut her own heart out rather than cause Richard any pain."

Helen shrugged. "Good point." To the waitress, "Another Irish coffee, and I'll take this half of my sandwich to go, and I'd like the apple pie, hot, if you please, with vanilla ice cream. MaryBeth?"

MaryBeth nodded. "The same." She eyed Enza's plate. "Are you going to finish that?"

Enza shook her head and pushed her plate away. "I don't think so."

MaryBeth brightened. "Excellent. Then I'll have hers to go as well. Thank you dear!"

Enza took a deep breath and looked at the two women, smiling happily as they finished their Irish coffees.

It was well worth the price of the lunch.

Jo sighed. "No permit for Bridezilla?"

Enza shook her head and looked at herself in the mirror. She was wearing well-cut jeans and a red cashmere V-neck sweater with soft, leather ballet flats. "How about this?" She asked.

Jo nodded. Enza invariably looked good in anything she put on. "Fine. What was the reason?"

Enza shrugged and pulled off the sweater. "No reason. I think that no one had ever needed to trot six horses down Main Street before, so there had never been a reason to grant the permit." She slipped a cobalt blue, sleeveless silk blouse over her head. "Is this better?"

"It's a good color, but I like the red," Jo said. She tried to steer her partner back to business. "What about a parade?"

Enza frowned at her reflection, then transferred the frown to Jo. "What are you talking about?"

"A parade." Jo had given the Basking Ridge bride situation a great deal of thought. After all, that was her job—to find a way to make Enza's promises to the client come true. "Maybe we could get a parade permit."

Enza thought, then nodded. "Excellent idea. I'll go back tomorrow morning." She pulled off the blue and slid into a long, white tunic of crinkled linen. "This? Do I look saintly and pure?"

Jo cackled. "With those boobs? Are you kidding? You wouldn't look saintly with wings."

Enza turned sideways and narrowed her eyes. "Yeah, they're still out there," she said. "Maybe a dress?"

"This is a casual dinner, no? Keep it simple."

Enza nodded and looked down at her feet. "Different shoes?"

Jo grinned. She had not seen Enza in such a state over a simple date in...ever. "I've seen you in your stilettos, and they send a distinct message. Are you sure you want to go there?"

Enza shook her head. "Oh, honey, don't get me started. It's been a while, and he is one fine-looking gentleman." She peeled off her jeans and tugged on black leggings. "Well?"

"Jeans are better." Jo sat back on against the headboard of Enza's king-sized bed. She was going against her better judgment, but was curious. "What were you saying about Faith's money?"

Off with the leggings, back on with the jeans. "Faith was loaded, and maybe held the purse strings. Molly was not happy about it, apparently."

"I wonder who gets it all," Jo muttered. She narrowed her eyes at Enza. "You need a necklace or something with the white. Or a scarf?"

"Richard gets the money? Who else is there? I'm betting Linda doesn't get it." Enza arranged a pale gray scarf around her neck.

"Well, it plays down the boobs," Jo said. She tugged at the ends of her hair. "Money is a pretty big motive too, you know?"

Enza shook her head and removed the scarf. "That would make Richard the prime suspect, and I find that very hard to believe. I'm interested in hearing what Lloyd finds out."

"Yeah, about that." Jo shifted her position on Enza's bed. "Isn't that all just a little too weird?"

"Phyl and Lloyd? Well, yeah. I mean, I always figured there was more to her than all that goody-goody earth-mother stuff. She's an unusual woman, our Phyllis. And Lloyd is a very unusual man."

Jo twisted a strand of red hair around her finger. "The missing Hummels are worrisome."

Enza went back to her walk-in closet and emerged with three pairs of shoes, all with very high heels. "I know. Did Molly sell them? Stash them? Use them to finance a paid assassin?" She slid her feet into black patent stilettos, instantly adding three inches to her height.

"What about Trulove? And you look like a hooker in those shoes."

Enza stepped out of the stilettos. "I'd love to know what he and Richard were arguing about. Something about being in deep. How about these? She looked critically down at her feet, in red pumps with a peek-a-boo toe.

"Only if you wear the white. The polish on your toes clashes with the red of your sweater. What did Trulove say again? Exactly?"

"That he was on board. But on board with what?" Enza took off the pumps and buckled herself into nude sandals with a four-inch heel. "How about the sandals?"

"I never understood sandals with a heel that high. What good would they be walking in the sand?"

Enza turned around and narrowed her eyes at the view from the rear. "These might work. And it's not about walking in the sand, Jo. It's never about sand." She faced forward again. "What was he on board with? Killing Faith?" She pulled off the tunic and slipped on the red sweater. "There."

"You look gorgeous." She always looked gorgeous, Jo thought. But she was not always practical. "How are you going to walk? What if he's on the second floor?"

Enza swore briefly and unbuckled the sandals, sliding

her feet once again into the ballet flats. "I think we need to talk to Mr. Trulove. Weren't you thinking about moving around some investments?"

Jo shook her head. "No, as a matter of fact, I was not."

"I bet Trulove would be able to give you some great advice."

"I take advice from my brother." Jo countered.

"Second opinions are always good."

"Why don't *you* talk to Mr. Trulove? Don't you have investments?"

Enza pushed back her hair, twisted for another back view, then nodded her head in satisfaction. "This is good."

"That's exactly what you were wearing when I got here."

"Yes. I should always trust my first instinct. But I can't talk to Mr. Trulove. I'll be too busy trying to become BFFs with Linda Hollowach." She glanced at her watch. "I gotta go. Thanks for the advice."

Jo sighed and watched her friend adjust the gold, dangling earrings. "Glad I could help."

SHE HAD four bottles of wine, a pound of cannoli and her perfume was just right. Enza Biondi approached Connor Ives' condo with the strength and confidence of a gladiator.

He opened the door wearing a tight black V-neck T-shirt, low-slung jeans and bare feet. His hair was still damp, and his jaw was faintly blue-black with stubble. She almost melted into the welcome mat.

He reached to take the tote bags of wine. "How many of us are there again?" He asked, his eyes twinkling. "Or are you going to try to get me drunk so that you can take advantage of me?"

She followed him through a short hallway, carrying her

cannoli. "If I have to get you drunk to take advantage of you," she said, "I'll consider the night a total failure."

He laughed as he set down the tote bags and pulled out each bottle of wine. He looked at the labels and whistled softly. "I'm impressed. You have excellent taste."

"In all things," she cooed. She pointed. "Open that one now. It needs to breathe."

She stepped around the high counter of his kitchen and walked across the living room to a brick patio, surrounded by a high, brick wall. In the center was a small table, draped in a long, white cloth, carefully set. There were even candles.

"This looks lovely," she said. She turned and glanced around the living room. The walls were painted a dark green, the couch was taupe, and the side chairs sage green. There was lots of dark wood, oil paintings and books. She nodded in approval.

"Not what you expected?" Connor asked.

"Not at all. Where's the life-sized poster of Dillinger?"

He waggled his eyebrows. "In my bedroom. I'll show you later."

She rolled her eyes in mock despair. "Such a tease."

He had the bottle and two glasses on a tray with a small bowl of something that looked crispy and light. He walked onto the patio and set the tray on a low table in front of a faux-wicker couch, tucked along the brick wall of the court-yard, under a potted palm. Enza followed, sat, and watched him as he poured.

She picked up her glass. "To this evening," she said, and clinked his glass. His eyes held hers for a moment, then he grinned, and they both drank.

"So, tell me," Enza said.

He lifted his shoulders, waited a long second, then let them drop. "Tell you what?"

"Well, to start, what's for dinner?"

He took another sip. "I know you said you were a steak kind of girl, but I decided to go with a simple cassoulet. It's been in the oven since this morning, and it's just now done. I bought some excellent bread to have with dinner. I also picked up a favorite cheese of mine in case we feel the need to snack on something later tonight." His lips twitched. "Kind of a just-in-case impulse buy."

"I see." The wine was luscious, and it slid down her throat like butter. "Next?"

He sat back and shrugged. "What else do you want to know?"

"Do you like your job?"

He nodded. "Very much. I've been with the Bureau about eighteen years. They recruited me while I was at Columbia, working on my law degree. I was a cop at the time, a detective in Narcotics." He drank. "Now, your turn."

She made a face. "I love my job, too. I was selling commercial real estate in Brooklyn right after my divorce and felt the need for a real change. I moved, as my sainted mother still refers to it, out to the Wild West. Jersey. Found Morristown, liked it, bought a building, and started an event planning business. Since my kids were all out of the house, it gave me a chance to baby something again. My daughter calls Luxe her little sister."

"How long have you been divorced?"

"Eight years. You?"

"Ten." He emptied his glass and leaned forward to pour some more. "Eight years is a long time. Didn't you get...lonely?"

She stretched out her arm and he added wine to her glass. "Here's the thing, Connor. I really like men, but I've got a very full life, and I'm very happy with it. Besides my business, I've got good friends and a few worthwhile causes to spend time with. I meet men pretty much every day of the week. Lonely really isn't something that's an active verb for me, you know?" She tilted her head. "You, though, seem to have the lonely angle covered."

He laughed. "Yes, well, the guys in the band tend to exaggerate my, ugh, success rate. Although I do meet an unusually high number of women at the places we play. And most of them are willing. And able. But I try not to give in to every invitation."

She grinned at him. "Would you have given into mine?"

He grinned back. "We're here, aren't we?"

"True. But we haven't even gotten through dessert."

"Well." He put down his glass and shifted his body until he was facing her. His arm slid along the back of the couch until it was behind her shoulders. "We could forgo the food altogether."

She shifted as well until they were face to face, the space between their bodies mere inches. She felt her pulse start to race. "But you went through all that trouble with the cassoulet."

"Yes, but the thing about a cassoulet is that the longer it bakes in the oven, the better it tastes."

She took her finger and ran it along the rough denim covering his thigh. "So, giving it another few minutes would actually make for a better-tasting dinner?"

His mouth twitched. "A few *minutes*? Now, I'm insulted."

She replaced her fingertip with her hand and squeezed gently. "I'll apologize. After."

He leaned forward and kissed her very gently on the lips. "Follow me."

And she did.

"THIS CASSOULET IS AMAZING," Connor said.

Enza took a bite, chewed thoughtfully, and swallowed. "Agreed. Very wise of you to let it cook that extra hour. I'm sure it wouldn't have been nearly as good if we'd eaten it before, you know..."

"I told you," Connor said with a grin, "I'm an excellent cook."

She grinned back. "Yes, you are."

Connor had his jeans back on. Enza was wearing his T-shirt. She thought for a moment of all the time she spent putting together the perfect outfit, which was now in a pile on Connor's bedroom floor.

Worth all the effort, she reasoned.

"More wine?" Connor offered.

"Yes, please." She dipped the crust of the bread into her bowl then maneuvered it into her mouth. She closed her eyes as she ate, then sighed.

"Enza, I think you enjoy eating almost as much as you enjoy—"

She opened her eyes and smiled. "Yes, you're right. Some days it's a very narrow margin."

Connor stared for a second, then threw back his head and laughed. When he was done he lifted himself from his chair, leaned across the table, and grabbed Enza by the back of her neck. He drew her forward until their lips met, giving her a deep, slow kiss. Then, he dropped back in his chair. He picked up his fork and waved it in the air. "I'll try to step up my game,"

Enza had to clear her throat. "Yeah, you do that."

She hadn't felt this good in a very long time. Excellent

sex was one thing. Excellent sex with a man who also had her laughing, then finishing off the evening with a delicious meal? Well, that was something altogether different.

She took another mouthful of cassoulet and heard her phone ring. Where was her phone? She looked around and followed Connor's pointing finger to the couch. She got up, dived into her purse, and pulled out her phone. It was Phyl. And it was almost nine o'clock at night, which was, Enza knew, practically Phyl's bedtime.

"Phyl, is something wrong?"

"What? No, not at all. But Lloyd and I had some news to share, so we went over to the office, but you're not here. Is everything OK?"

"Yes. I'm with Connor. What's up?"

Enza could hear Phyl's muffled voice, obviously talking to Lloyd.

"We'll be right over."

"Over where? Who's we?" Enza yelped, but the connection was gone.

She looked at Connor. "Your uncle and my partner are on the way over," she said, getting up off the couch. "I guess I should get dressed."

Connor followed her into the bedroom. "My uncle and who?"

Enza picked up her jeans and shook them out. "Phyllis. My business partner. I told you about their deep and unbreakable connection. She and Lloyd have joined forces to help." She stepped into her panties and pulled off his T-shirt.

He closed his eyes. "I warned you about him."

"Yes, you did, but I need inside help if I'm going to find out who murdered Faith McGowan."

His eyes popped open. "What?"

She was adjusting her bra straps. "I just asked Lloyd if he had any, you know, contacts."

"Contacts where?" He was so annoyed, he almost didn't stare at her breasts.

"The police department, of course," Enza said, sliding the red sweater over her shoulders. She bent to pull on her jeans. Connor closed his eyes again.

"Enza, what are you talking about? "

"I'm talking about a few things I found out about Molly McGowan, and her son, and how Faith controlled all the money, and Molly may have guessed she was headed for the nursing home."

"Enza, the police know what they're doing. Why do you feel the need to interfere?" He opened his eyes again. Thankfully, she was now fully clothed and was standing in front of the mirror. But the way her fingers were raking through her hair...

She snagged his T-shirt off the bed and threw it at him. "You should probably put this on. Can I tell you? Your body is kinda a turn-on right now, and I don't think we have enough time for another round. Are you trying to torture me here?" She took one last look in the mirror, then brushed past him. "By the way, you're getting a bit of an erection there, and as flattered as I am, I really don't think we have enough time to do anything productive about it. Just sayin'." She winked. "Next time."

THEY WERE SITTING at the kitchen counter, fully clothed, when Lloyd and Phyllis arrived. Phyl was in one of her non-work outfits — black leggings with pink flamingos on them, and a loose, flowing black tunic that fell to her knees. She paused for a moment when Connor answered the door, then held out a hand.

"It's a pleasure to see you again, Connor," she said demurely, then pulled her hand from his to sweep past, crossing over to Enza, and giving her a kiss on the cheek. "Enza, you look lovely, as usual. I hope you had a good evening.

Enza kept a straight face. "I had a wonderful cassoulet. And interesting conversation of course. You?"

Phyl dimpled. "Lloyd and I experimented in my claw-foot tub. Very satisfactorily."

Lloyd, however, looked as though he'd been stretched thin. Connor looked down at the older man in concern.

"Uncle, are you OK?"

Lloyd nodded and looked around. "A glass of something, perhaps?" he asked, sinking into the couch.

Enza sighed. "Let me guess, Lloyd. You let Phyllis drive over?"

He nodded weakly and stretched out a shaking hand to take the glass of whiskey from Connor. "Oh, yes."

Enza grinned wickedly. "Bet that's the last time for that, right Lloyd?"

He closed his eyes as he swallowed, then nodded reverently. "Oh, yes. Never again in the night. During daylight, it's, well, a bit tricky, of course, but at night..." He shuddered.

Phyl waved a hand. "Lloyd was very thoughtful, letting me drive. And he didn't have a word of criticism."

"He was probably shocked speechless," Enza cracked. "So, Lloyd, what did you find out?"

He opened his eyes, held out his glass, and cleared his throat. "There were no whatcha-call, Hummel things found. I'm trying to find out if there was any significant activity in or out of Molly's investment accounts recently." He downed the contents of his glass in one quick gulp.

Connor, his own glass of Jameson halfway to his lips, froze. "How do you intend to find that out?"

Lloyd, fortified by Jameson, looked resolute. "Now, Connor, that would be telling."

Connor exhaled loudly. "You do remember that I am a sworn law enforcement official?"

"Of course, my boy. That's why I won't be revealing any of my sources." Relaxed now, Lloyd patted the place beside him on the couch. Phyl floated over in a swirl of black gauze. "Now Enza, this is what we know. Molly had a few thousand dollars in a savings account and her funeral was pre-paid. Until she moved in with Richard, she'd been living in a very nice one-bedroom near downtown in Madison, paid for by Faith, and a two thousand dollar a month allowance. Faith again. After her fall, she spent a few months in rehab before trying to live on her own again, with no success. So, she moved in with Richard and Faith, and the allowance went down to one hundred dollars a week."

"Do we know where Faith got her money?" Enza asked.

Lloyd nodded. "Her godmother was very wealthy and left Faith everything. That was quite a while ago. Twenty years? Anyway, Faith became very rich sometime after she and Richard married."

Enza chewed her lower lip, thinking. "Godmother? Did Linda also inherit?"

Lloyd shook his head. "Not a cent."

Enza nodded to herself. "Interesting," she muttered. "Cannoli anyone?"

Phyl waved. "Yes, please! I hate to ask, but is there coffee?"

Connor bowed his head, the perfect host. "I can make some espresso, or would you prefer regular?"

Phyl beamed. "Espresso. Thank you, you're very sweet."

Enza glanced over and saw Connor's mouth twitch in amusement.

"I'll help," she offered.

There were a few minutes of hurried activity, and when they all settled again, each had a plate with a fresh cannoli and a small cup of espresso. Lloyd had requested, and gotten, a shot of Jameson in his.

"So," Enza said, crossing her legs and nibbling the edge of her pastry, "Linda must have really hated her sister?"

Lloyd lifted both eyebrows. "That, my dear, is speculation. I would say yes, but you should probably get some sort of confirmation."

"What else have you got?" Enza asked.

Lloyd glanced briefly at Connor. "No fingerprints were found on the knife. And the doorknob to the study had been wiped clean. Richard is the number one suspect right now. After all, he's the one who inherits everything."

"Was she stabbed from behind?"

Lloyd shook his head. "Whoever did it was standing right in front of her."

Enza sniffed. "So, that rules out someone sneaking up on her. And with no defensive wounds..." She lifted an eyebrow at Lloyd, who shook his head.

"None," he said.

Connor sank deeper into his chair, muttering.

Phyl shook her head. "Richard makes no sense. Look at all the money Faith was willing to give toward Molly. She was probably paying for the nursing home. He already was getting everything, wasn't he?"

Lloyd shrugged. "There are a couple of theories, the first

being that he wanted his mother to continue to live with him, not in a home."

"I can guarantee," Enza said, "that theory is from someone who has *not* met Molly McGowan."

Phyl sighed and shook her head. "Never underestimate the mother-son bond."

Enza snorted. "That's bull. Faith was a warm and lovely woman who was a pleasure to live with. Molly is a shrew."

Connor lifted his head. "Never assume what you see is the truth, Enza. Faith appeared to be a warm and lovely woman who was a pleasure to live with. That has nothing to do with who she really was, or what her marriage to Richard was like. For all you know, Faith could have been a sadistic sociopath who had her husband and mother-in-law living in fear."

Lloyd shook his finger. "Excellent point, my boy. Another reason for Richard to have killed her."

Enza narrowed her eyes at Connor. "I thought this wasn't your case."

"It's not. But I happen to be the only trained professional in the room. I thought you might benefit from my expertise."

Enza smiled. "You're right there, Connor. And may I say I find your expertise *very* beneficial."

He ducked his head, blushing.

Phyl licked a smidge of coffee off her upper lip. "Am I missing something?"

Enza shook her head. "Nope. Thanks for the info, Lloyd. We need to think about this."

Phyl raised her hand and waved. "I think what we need to do is try to find out where those Hummel figurines went. After all, when you're looking for motive, follow the money. In this case, the lack of it. Those little trinkets were worth a bundle, and now they're gone. I bet that's important."

Lloyd nodded slowly. "Yes, darlin', you're probably right. What kind of market is there for those sort of things? Pawnshop? E-bay?"

"Speaking of money," Connor said, "wasn't there a banker at the party?"

Enza finished off her espresso. "Yes, but I've already got Jo on the case there. What I need is eyes on the ground at Linda's place. That's where Richard and Molly are staying. I'd love to know what's going on there."

Connor tilted his head. "Jo is on *what* case?"

Enza stood up and shook down her sweater. Connor felt his mouth go dry.

"I think we should go. Phyl, can I give you a lift? Or..." She looked meaningfully at Lloyd.

Lloyd shook his head. "I'm thinkin' I'll be spending the night with Connor here. I don't drink and drive, you know."

Enza grinned. "Yes, I know. Okay, Phyl, let's go."

Connor walked the two women outside and watched as Phyl slid into the passenger side of the car. He draped his arm around Enza's shoulder as they walked to the other side of the car.

"Are we going to see each other again?" he asked.

She leaned against the side of the car and pulled him close. "I certainly hope so," she murmured. "I had a *lovely* time." Her eyes were dancing.

He bent to give her a long, deep kiss her lips. "I'm in DC until Friday night. I'll call you when I'm back."

"I'll pencil you in," she said, pushing him away, getting into her car and backing out slowly.

Phyl waited until they were out on the street.

"Did you sleep with that young man?"

Enza looked sideways at her. "What do you think?"

Phyl sighed. "About time. I was worried about you drying up."

Enza gave her a look. "I was worrying the same thing about you."

Phyl settled herself back in her seat. "Don't you worry about me, Enza. I'm doing quite well, thank you very much. And Connor? An excellent choice."

Enza grinned. "Yeah. I know."

6

Miles Trulove looked carefully over the single sheet of paper that Jo had handed to him. "Hmmm."

Jo leaned forward from her perch on the edge of the soft, cushy chair opposite Trulove's wide, sleek desk. "Is that a good hmmm? Or a bad hmmm?"

Trulove cleared his throat. "Neither, actually. I just never encountered a person with six different saving accounts before."

Jo shrugged. "My brother's idea. He's very conservative when it comes to money."

"Yes," Trulove agreed. "Very conservative. But leaving this much money in saving accounts and CD's is...not very forward thinking. You could be using your money to make *more* money. That's how it usually works."

Jo nodded in agreement. "That's what I thought. So when I met you the other day, even under such extreme circumstances, I thought that maybe you could advise me of a better approach."

Trulove cleared his throat. "Usually, Miss Collins..."

"Call me Jo. Please."

"Yes. Jo. Usually a person with this much income has some sort of retirement plan. Do you?"

She shook her head.

"Any additional investments?"

She shook her head again. "Just what's there."

"Well. First, let me tell you that you could be doing much better, investment-wise. Penny stocks usually don't guarantee much of a return."

She shrugged. She had spent her twenties paying off her student loans, and never had enough money to actually worry about. When she began working with Enza, she had, for the first time, a little extra at the end of every month, but no idea what to do with it. Which was why she listened to her brother and then stopped thinking about it. "My brother thinks that there's less of a chance of my losing money with those."

"True. But there's also less of a chance that you'll *make* money. There is a certain risk, of course, but generally speaking, investing in mixed stock and bond funds is, long term, the way to go. And we'll get some sound stocks for you to purchase outright, set up an Individual Retirement Account, and perhaps some annuities. How does that sound?"

Jo brightened. "That sounds like just what I need. After all, I've got thirty, maybe forty years ahead of me before I retire, and I want to be able to laze around in my golden years. Maybe on an island somewhere." She waved a hand. "You know, with a devoted housekeeper. And a pool boy."

Trulove smiled. "Sounds perfect." He then launched into a very long and complicated explanation of her options. Jo found her head spinning after the first minute, so she let herself go on autopilot and alternated between looking at

Trulove with a fixed expression of complete interest and thinking about the pictures on the wall. Abstract watercolors that did not at all go with the dark, heavy furniture in the room.

As her eyes wandered, she caught glimpse of a group of framed photographs, high on the shelf just above Trulove's head. The McGowan's. And was that the sister? Linda? Why on earth would he have a picture of Linda? Especially one of her with her head tilted just so, a saucy smile and lots of airbrushed smoky eye?

She brought her eyes back to his face. Yes, he was still talking, but obviously winding down.

"...which will, of course, give you complete control, but still allowing us the freedom to make those important decisions for you. How does that sound?"

She smiled. It had to be better than what she had going on now, which was a trickle of interest payments that barely covered a nice dinner out on the town. "Sounds like just what I need. Where do I sign?"

He tut-tutted. "Well, you won't be signing anything today. We'll put together a plan, get all the necessary paperwork together and you can come back, sometime next week?"

She nodded and stood up, holding out her hand. "Absolutely. I can't thank you enough. This is a big moment for me, getting all financially responsible and all."

He stood as well and grasped her hand in both of his. "My pleasure. Really."

She shifted her gaze. "That picture behind you, is that the McGowan's?"

He turned and took down the silver frame, looking at it as though he'd forgotten it had even been there. "Yes. I've known Richard quite a long time. This is such a tragedy. He and Faith were devoted to each other."

She reached out a hand. "May I?"

He gave her the picture.

Faith looked much younger, as did Trulove, but Richard looked almost the same as when she'd seen him just four days ago. "Richard hasn't changed at all," she said.

Trulove nodded. "Yes. I sometimes joke that he's made a pact with the devil."

She arched one brow. "You mean Molly?"

He cracked a smile. "No, but you're right, she's a tough old bird."

"I gathered she and Faith did not get along?"

He walked around his desk to get closer to her. "To tell you the truth," he said, leaning toward her and dropping his voice, "Faith had reached the end of her rope. Molly had become impossible to live with. Poor Richard, to be caught between those two women." He shook his head. "My heart goes out to him, of course, but at least now he doesn't have to make the agonizing decision to send Molly away."

"I thought," Jo said slowly, "that Richard was on board with that."

He looked at her sharply, taking the photo back.

"Just something he said," Jo hurried on. "I probably misinterpreted. I do that a lot."

Trulove raised his eyebrows. "Richard would have been happy to have Molly continue to live there. He was devoted to her. It was all Faith. And it was, I must say, the only thing I ever saw the two of them argue about." He stepped back and carefully repositioned the photograph.

"And that's...Faiths sister?" Jo asked and pointed to another frame on a higher shelf.

"Yes," Trulove said, somewhat abruptly. "Now, if you just see my assistant, and set up something for next week?"

"Certainly," Jo said, smiling again. "Next week."

WHEN JO ENTERED the Luxe offices, she heard two very distinct things. Someone humming a happy, lilting tune, and low, angry voices behind the closed door of Enza's office.

She took a quick peek into the living room/lounge, and saw Lloyd, sitting on the couch, flipping through *Brides* magazine, humming.

"Hey," she said. "You alone?"

Lloyd lifted his eyes and jerked his head toward Enza's office. "Phyl and I got here a bit ago. They're having a...meeting."

Jo turned and walked back to Enza's office. She put her ear against the wooden door. Muffled, but still angry. She knocked once, then turned the knob.

Enza and Phyl were standing in the middle of the crowded office, nose to nose. They both glared at Jo as she entered.

"Lloyd said we were having a meeting?" Jo said.

Enza threw up her hands and tramped around her desk, dropped into her chair, and glared some more. "Phyl thinks we should hire Lloyd," she grumbled.

Jo carefully closed the door behind her. "To do what?"

"Well," Phyl said brightly, "for one thing, the man in a mechanical genius. He could fix all the things around here that have been just sitting there, broken."

"Like what?" Jo asked.

Phyl spread her arms, "Well, you know, things. Like the back door window that has been cracked for years."

"That crack is half an inch long," Enza pointed out through gritted teeth.

"Still," Phyl plowed on, "it should be repaired. And then there's always the need for lifting and such at our functions. We all know how heavy those carts can be."

"We've managed those carts for over three years now, Phyl." Jo pointed out.

"True," Phyl countered. "But I'm not getting any younger, you know. None of us are. Lloyd would be more suited to handle them."

"Lloyd is older than all of us, and, not to sound harsh, is so scrawny I doubt he could manage a full shopping cart at Target," Enza said. "And most of our functions are on the weekends, and you just told me he has his music gigs on the weekends, so he wouldn't be around to help anyway."

Phyl nodded. "True. But during the week, think how helpful it would be to have him around."

Enza fixed her stare on Jo. "Phyl wants us to put her boyfriend on the payroll so he can work at his convenience, not ours. And she wants to pay him twice what we're paying the girls."

"The girls won't have to do any more heavy lifting," Phyl argued.

"But they're not complaining," Enza shot back. "Why should we pay someone twice as much to do the exact same work we're paying the girls now if they're not complaining? If Lloyd needs another job, I don't see why we should have to give it to him just because you think he's so friggin' wonderful. You've known him less than a week. I'm still waiting for him to show his true colors and start sticking silverware in his pockets."

Phyl's face turned red. "That's unfair!"

"How do you know? You don't know him at all Phyl.

Maybe you have a shared destiny with the man, but that has nothing to do with Luxe Affairs. Don't drag Jo and me into it."

Phyl clenched her teeth and crossed her arms tightly against her chest. "Our personal relationship has nothing to do with this."

Enza rocked back in her chair. "Are you friggin' kidding me? Like, you would really just come up to me and suggest we hire someone for a job he's never done before at twice the amount of money we're paying our experienced team if you just ran into him at Starbucks? Get real, Phyl."

Phyl sniffed and turned to Jo. "What do you think?"

Jo backed against the wall. "Well, I think Enza has a point. About weekends. That's when we could use the help. I mean, look at this week. Just two events, both fairly small and manageable with our regular crew. But next weekend, we're packing in three events and we could use extra help." She lifted her chin. "And Lloyd doesn't look terribly...strong."

"He's got amazing energy," Phyl argued.

"That may be," Jo soothed. "But if he can't work when we *need* him..."

Phyl moved her shoulders around and looked between Jo and Enza. "I suppose I can't argue with *both* of you," she muttered.

Enza closed her eyes tightly and took a few cleansing breaths. "Then I hope we can consider this matter settled." She cleared her throat. "Since this is apparently a meeting, do we have any new business?"

Phyl rolled her eyes. Jo raised her hand.

"According to Miles Trulove, Richard did not want Molly to move into a nursing home. It was Faith's idea, and apparently they fought about it."

Enza sat up. "Really? What else did he say?"

"That a balanced portfolio of stocks and bonds will give me the best return in the long term."

Phyl snorted. "Well, everyone knows *that*."

Jo shrugged. "I didn't. I thought I was doing well with interest from my Select Savings accounts."

Enza rapped on her desk with her knuckles. "What else did he say about the McGowan's?"

"That was it. He's known them a long time. There was a picture of them on his shelf. Richard has a painting of himself in an attic somewhere, cause he hasn't aged in years. There was also a picture of Linda. Framed."

Enza lifted an eyebrow. "Now, that's interesting." Her mind started churning. They hadn't seemed to even know each other at the party. In fact, she'd assumed they'd never met. But he had her picture?

Jo sat down across from Enza. "Did Lloyd find out anything?"

"Faith controlled the money that went to Molly," Phyl said. "And once Molly moved out of her own place, that allowance was cut drastically."

"We also need to find out where all those expensive Hummels disappeared to. They were worth a bundle," Enza said. "Although the simple answer could be that Molly needed the extra money once her allowance was cut."

"But what would she need it *for*?" Phyl asked. "She was getting her room and board free, she didn't have a car, and I doubt she spent lots of money on clothes. What would she need that much cash for?"

Enza nodded. "Good point. God, I wish we could talk to Richard. Or Molly." She chewed her lower lip. "And I wish we could find out more about Faith. Connor is right. We only have one view of her, and people are rarely only one thing. I bet there was another side that wasn't so perfect."

Jo grinned. "Yeah, Connor...how'd that go last night?"

"Fine," Enza said smoothly. "He's an excellent cook."

At that moment, the phone rang. Enza picked up and dropped her voice into her professional mode.

"Luxe Affairs. This is Enza, how may we help you today?" She listened, then her eyebrows shot up. She grabbed a pen, scribbled, and practically bounced up and out of her chair. Her voice, however, remained calm. "Why, thank you for this. I appreciate it very much, especially during such a trying time."

She put down the phone and grinned triumphantly. "That was Molly McGowan. She wants us to pick up our last check. And here's Linda's address." She pointed at Phyl. "You come with me, Phyl. I think Molly hated you least."

Jo stood, sputtering. "What should I do?"

Enza grabbed her purse. "Well, if you want, you can go out there and tell Lloyd he won't be working for us."

Jo shook her head. "Nope, that's on Phyl."

LINDA HOLLOWACH LIVED in a townhouse in Parsippany, quite nice, but Enza couldn't help but think that Molly would consider it a step down from Richard's home in Upper Montclair. Although, to be honest, pretty much anything would be a step down. Aside from, perhaps, something from the Gilded Age.

Molly opened the door and led them through a small living room to an even smaller kitchen, where Virginia Crewe sat, sipping a cup of tea. She squeezed in at a round table and gestured for Enza and Phyl to do the same.

Phyl leaned over, grasped Molly's hand, and patted it gently. "How are you holding up?" she asked.

Molly jerked her hand away. "I'm fine, thank you very much. Terrible business, of course, but this is my son's loss, not mine."

Phyl turned to Virginia. "You were at the party too, weren't you? Such an awful thing. How are you?"

Virginia smiled weakly. "Managing."

Enza rearranged her expression to hide her surprise. What was Virginia doing here, hanging around the grieving widower?

Virginia stood. "I know you have business to attend to, Molly," she said. "I'll just be in the living room."

Molly nodded and watched her leave. Then, she moved her shoulders around and folded her hands. "I understand we'd be owing you some money?"

Enza nodded. "Yes. We usually get paid at the end of the event."

Molly lowered her eyes to the tabletop. "At the end of the event, my daughter-in-law was dead," she said carefully.

Enza made a noise, forcing Molly's eyes up. "And if that had anything to do with the services we provided, it might be relevant to this discussion. But since the two are totally unrelated..."

Molly raised her eyebrows. "Richard did leave a check."

"He's at work?" Enza asked.

"Well, of course he's at work," Molly countered. "You don't think he'd be lyin' up in his bed, weepin', did you?"

"Of course not," Phyl soothed.

"But, maybe he's with the police?" Enza asked.

Molly's sharp eyes narrowed. "The police are clueless," she snapped. "I have a very strong feeling that they will never find out who did this terrible thing."

Enza shifted in her seat. "I don't know, Molly. It's not like a total stranger came in and killed Faith. There's a limited pool of suspects, and eventually, someone is going to crack." Unless, Enza thought, Molly did it. She couldn't imagine Molly ever cracking under any pressure.

There was a noise of the front door opening and closing, and Linda Hollowach came in. She bent to kiss Molly on the cheek, then sat next to her, looking at the two women from Luxe with vague distaste.

"I suppose you're here to get paid?" Linda said.

"Yes, as a matter of fact, we are," Enza said. "But I also wanted to see how you all were doing. Molly here seems, miraculously, to be just fine. How are *you* doing?"

Linda, without carefully applied make-up and styled hair, looked more like Faith: pleasant but not beautiful. She shrugged. "Faith and I had our differences. But she was my sister, and of course I loved her."

"Of course," repeated Enza.

Linda glanced up sharply. "I don't know who you are, but you seem to be the sort of person who feels like they can make assumptions about things you know nothing about."

"Actually, I'm not that sort of person at all," Enza said. "I'm the sort of person who looks and listens very carefully. To all sorts of things. Like how your sister was not at all happy to see you when you arrived at the party."

Linda sniffed. "We'd been having a disagreement."

"About what?" Enza asked.

Linda drew back. "I don't see where that's any of your business."

"Faith was my client. I liked her," Enza said. "I've been talking to the police, trying to help them find out who did this. You *do* want to find out who did this, don't you?"

Molly and Linda exchanged a look, and Enza felt something in her stomach curl. "What do you know, Linda?" she asked quietly.

Linda stood up so abruptly that her chair bounced back and fell to the floor. "I want you to leave," she said coldly.

"Sure," Enza said easily. "As soon as I get the check."

Molly and Linda exchanged another look.

"I cannot believe you want money from us," Molly said. "After all this."

Enza leaned forward, thoroughly pissed off now. "Listen, lady, you called us, remember? We have a signed contract with Richard, he owes us, and it seems like you're trying to guilt us out of a lot of money. Now, why would you do that? Do you need that money for something else?"

Linda was breathing hard and fast. "Give her the check," she muttered.

Molly frowned. "Linda, dear, I thought you—"

"Give her the check," Linda said louder.

Molly looked up at her, still frowning, then slid her hand into the pocket of her skirt and brought forth a folded check.

Enza opened it. It was made out for the correct amount, and signed, but the 'Pay To' line was blank. "This is not made out to us," she said slowly.

Molly cleared her throat. "I told Richard I wasn't sure about the company name. I, ah, asked him to leave it blank."

Enza looked at Molly. "So, if you hadn't given it to me..." She looked up at Linda. "You two would have, what? Just cashed this yourselves?"

Linda's face was flaming red. "Leave. Now."

"What on earth did you need this money for, Linda?" Enza asked quietly. "We're not talking thousands and thousands of dollars here. What's going on?"

Linda turned and practically ran from the kitchen. Molly folded her hands and looked down at them.

"I think perhaps you should be going," she said.

"Molly," Phyl said softly. "Is there anything you want to tell us?"

Molly raised her eyes, and they were full of tears. "She was going to turn me out," she said. "Put me in one of those...places. I'd never see my son, never be able to entertain my friends, I'd be locked up in some horrible place..."

"Molly, what are you talking about?" Phyl said. "A nursing home? Those places are like resorts now. You probably would have had a little apartment all to yourself, with someone to cook and clean for you...why, some places I've seen are nicer than where I'm living right now! Who put an idea like that in your head?"

Molly's lower lip quivered. "Go. Both of you."

Enza stood and slipped the check into her purse. She and Phyl walked out of the kitchen and through the living room. As they got to the front door, they heard a rough cough behind them. Linda was standing on the stairs.

"I don't want to see or hear from the two of you again," she said in a low and hoarse voice. "You've caused enough trouble around here."

"How is that, Linda?" Enza said. "By asking questions?"

Linda turned and went silently up the stairs.

Virginia had been huddled in a chair, but now stood up and approached, looking meek and frail. "I know you probably told the police about the argument Faith and I had, but believe me, it meant nothing," she said.

Enza narrowed her eyes. "It didn't sound like nothing, Virginia. And what are you doing here anyway? Is Molly lining you up already as a replacement?"

Molly swooped in from the kitchen like an avenging

angel. "What are you implying? Virginia is my dear friend. She's with me to lend comfort and support."

Enza snorted. Molly? In need of comfort and support? She had already made it clear she felt no loss. Her biggest fear had just been alleviated and Wife #2 was right there, waiting in the wings.

Molly went past them, her cane thumping, and dramatically threw open the front door. "Get out."

Enza and Phyl turned and found the doorway blocked by Richard, looking tired and a bit confused.

"Mother? What's going in here?"

Molly sniffed. "These ladies came by to get their money," she said, her voice full of distain. "And now they're leaving."

Enza reached over to touch Richard's sleeve. "I never got to talk to you...after. I am so sorry for your loss. Faith was lovely."

Richard's face went smooth, all emotion replaced by a bland handsomeness. "Thank you. Yes, my wife was one of a kind." His eyes went past Enza and narrowed as he saw Virginia Crewe.

Molly, watching his face, opened the door wider. "Come in, dear. I thought you were at work."

His face remained expressionless, but Enza saw a spark of something in his eyes. "I couldn't concentrate. Hello, Virginia. I didn't expect to see you here."

"She's keeping me company," Molly said in a rush. "I didn't want to be alone."

"Linda isn't here?" Richard asked, an edge to his voice as he went into the living room and dropped his briefcase on a chair.

"Well, yes," of course," Molly said, her tone changing. "But you know what a dear friend Ginny is."

"Yes," Richard said, sitting down slowly. "I do know."

The tension in the air was palpable, and Enza glanced at Phyl. "We're on our way out," she said, speaking directly to Richard. "Again, I'm sorry."

They hurried out and did not speak until they were back in Enza's car.

"What was that all about?" Phyl asked.

Enza shook her head as she started the car. "I have no idea."

"Was it just me," Phyl asked, "or did Virginia seem really uncomfortable in there?"

Enza tapped the steering wheel with her finger. "No, you're right. I don't think she wanted to be there at all. And what was with the money? They didn't want to pay us."

Phyl made a clucking sort of sound. "No. They didn't."

"I wonder why not. Did they need the money for themselves?" Enza said. "I think I need to talk to Detective Whalen again."

Phyl shook her head. "He's not going to be very happy about that."

"I don't care," Enza said grimly. "Linda and Molly know more than they're saying, and somebody needs to find out what that is."

DETECTIVE WHALEN SMILED at Enza as she approached and gestured for her to sit in a chair at the end of his desk. She looked around. "You don't have an office?"

His smile broadened. "The chief barely has an office. What can I do for you today? You said you had *more* information?"

Enza had changed from the jeans and sweater she'd been wearing earlier into a pale gray body-con dress and high black heels. She settled in and crossed one shapely leg over the other. "Did Molly tell you where all her figurines went?"

The detective managed not to look totally confused. "Figurines?"

"Yes. Apparently, she spent a great deal of her allowance on antique Hummel figurines, which are rare and some are worth thousands of dollars apiece. According to my sources, she had quite a few when she lived alone, but the collection had been missing in action after moving in with Richard. That meant that, sometime, she must have sold them for a great deal of money. Why would she need a great deal of money, do you think?"

Detective Whalen shook his head. "Your *sources*?"

"And yesterday, she tried to guilt me out of a very sizable check that Richard wrote, but left blank. She tried to get me to walk away, which meant she could have made it out to *herself.*"

"Yesterday? You saw Molly McGowan *yesterday?*"

Enza nodded. "She called me to tell me she had our final payment. We usually charge a third upon signing the contract, a third a week before, and the last third after the party. But after this party, well, I couldn't ask for a check, of course."

Detective Whalen nodded his head. "Of course." He looked up and saw his partner enter the room, and hastily waved him over.

"Jack, Ms. Biondi has just been telling me that Molly might have been hurting for money. Did you do the financials?"

Jack Newberry tried very hard not to stare at Enza's legs, and almost succeeded. "Yes. During the past six months, there was very little activity in her regular accounts, but she had some investments, and three large deposits, no pattern, and then seventy-five thousand dollars was taken out two weeks before the party."

Enza shot up, both feet hitting the floor, her heels making a loud noise that sent the squad room jumping. "The pay-off," she said.

Detectives Newberry and Whalen exchanged a look. "Pay-off for what?" Whalen asked.

"She paid someone to kill Faith, of course," Enza said. "She couldn't do it herself, so she paid somebody. Did anyone on her guest list have a rap sheet?"

"Ms. Biondi," Whalen said gently, "are you trying to suggest that Molly McGowan put a contract out on her daughter-in-law? And sold her collection of Hummel figurines to finance it?"

Enza nodded. "Of course. It makes perfect sense."

The two men exchanged another look, and Newberry shook his head. "Believe it or not, that's one theory we haven't even considered."

She settled back again, folded her arms deliberately under her breasts, crossed her legs again, and smiled sweetly. "What theories *have* you considered?"

Whalen leaned back in his chair to better take in the view. "Well, Trulove was very, ah, reticent to discuss his client's financial position. According to him, Richard was trying to add his name to some of Faith's accounts. Faith, apparently, didn't object, but couldn't understand the *why*. Richard has a fairly healthy salary on his own, but the bulk of the wealth is, that is, *was* hers."

"What about Molly? Did she have anything that Trulove was managing?"

Newberry shrugged. "Actually, yes. Trulove managed Molly's account when she lived on her own, paid the rent and all the bills, and released cash as Molly asked for it, all within the guidelines set by Faith. He said the terms were very generous but had significantly changed after she moved in with them. He also handled her personal investments, the same account that recently was relieved of seventy-five grand."

Enza nodded thoughtfully. "What did he say about that argument? The one I overheard and told you about? What was he on board with, exactly? Faith looking into things, or Richard keeping her from looking into things?"

Whalen spread his hands. "Trulove insisted that Faith had just asked why certain accounts were still active."

"And what was the answer to that?" Enza asked.

Newberry folded his arms. "Trulove was vague, but we decided not to push him on it. We have a warrant, and we'll know everything sooner or later. But believe me, we're going to have him in for another talk. He is a slippery kind of a guy."

Enza tapped her nails on the hard arm of the chair. "Can I listen?"

Whalen's eyebrows shot up. "To what?"

"When you talk to Trulove, of course," Enza answered sweetly.

Whalen stood up and picked up a few files that were on his desk. "Ms. Biondi, thank you very much for the, ah, additional information. And we do appreciate your interest, we really do. But no, you really can't listen in while we question witnesses."

"He's more than a witness," Enza said, arching one perfect eyebrow. "I bet he's a suspect."

Newberry reached down to place a hand on her shoulder. "All the more reason. Do you need me to show you out?"

"There's something else," she said.

Whalen sighed. "Why am I not surprised?"

Enza tried to look apologetic. "Virginia Crewe's scarf was left in Molly's room."

Newberry leaned forward. "When?"

Enza shrugged. "Sometime after her argument with Faith."

"And you know this...how?" Whalen asked.

Enza dug into her purse and pulled it out. "Because the other day when I was there, I found it on the floor of Molly's closet."

Whalen exhaled loudly. "You were snooping in Molly McGowan's room? That was a crime scene."

"There was no yellow tape across her doorway."

"There was yellow tape all around the whole house!" Whalen practically shouted. "You took evidence from a crime scene! I could have you arrested for that."

She rolled her eyes. "Really, Detective." She pointed her finger at the scarf. "That is a clue. Your people probably just thought it belonged to Molly, but I remember it quite clearly as being worn by Virginia Crewe, and she had it on right before Faith was killed. So why was she in Molly's closet? Or..." She sat up, her eyes bright. "Maybe Molly found it someplace really incriminating, and tried to hide it?" She looked excitedly from one police detective to the other, saw the looks on both faces, and slumped in the chair. "It's a clue. Are you really going to arrest me for finding a *clue*?"

"Ms. Biondi, I think you should leave." Whalen was taking deep breaths. "Right now."

Enza rolled her eyes and stood. She shook down her dress, causing at least one disconnected phone call, and smiled at the men. "I'll see my way out, gentlemen. And if I should hear anything else, I'll be sure to let you know."

"Hey, yeah..." Whalen began. "What about those sources of yours?"

She shook her head and smiled brightly. "A lady never tells." She walked away quickly, her heels echoing through the squad room.

A rookie officer, his third day on the job, slipped completely out of his chair and hit the floor with a crash.

ENZA GOT a text from Connor saying he was back and did she feel like a quick bite?

She texted back. *How quick? I have a breakfast meeting tomorrow for 75 very picky eaters*

Well, I have no food, so...

What kind of invite is that? Be over at 7 I'll bring Chinese.

She was late, mostly because Phyl was having her usual last-minute panic that there wouldn't be enough food for the morning's event, that the weather was going to be terrible, everyone would hate her French toast...

Lloyd was there, trying to soothe, but Phyl was beyond even his influence. Enza left her with Gina and Laurel, stopped by Hunan Kitchen for take-out, and drove to Connors.

He opened the door before she had a chance to ring the bell. "You really brought food?" he asked, taking the bag from her hands.

"Of course I did," she said, following him in. "What, you think I'm just here for sex?"

He pulled out a few containers. "Well, I was kinda hoping..."

She bumped him with one hip. "I need food. And I have a few questions."

He opened a cabinet to get plates, looking at her suspiciously. "Questions about what?"

"Why don't you have a buzz cut like most Feds?"

"Oh." He put forks on the counter and opened a container, spilling out beef in black bean sauce. "I'm not a field agent. I spend most of my time in a lab. The forensics lab."

"Here?"

"In New York. I take the train every day."

"Ah." She sat on a stool by the counter and took a bite. "Any chance of getting me a copy of the police interview with Richard McGowan?"

"*What?*" He put down his fork. "Are you kidding me?"

She shrugged. "Can't hurt to ask. Is there duck sauce?"

He bit half an egg roll. "I did talk to Whalen. Kind of off-the-record."

She licked her lips. "And?"

"There's not a clue to be found. Whoever did this left no trace."

"That's going to make this tough."

"It's already tough. The only people with anything against Faith were Molly and Linda, and both of them were pretty much in plain sight all afternoon."

"They don't see Virginia as a suspect?"

He shook his head. "No. For one thing, the woman is like a baby chick. Lacks the physical strength to plunge a knife through a human breastbone."

"But if she was angry enough? I've seen her with her adrenaline up, and it's impressive."

He shrugged. "Not impressive enough for Whalen. Molly and Linda are getting the scrutiny."

"Yeah, there's something going on with those two. Wine?"

"Oh. Sorry. What do you mean, going on?"

She watched him pour a glass, took a sip, and speared a snap pea on her fork. "They tried to guilt me out of my last payment. They had a check from Richard, without my name on it, and Molly was very reluctant to hand it over."

"What? You talked to them?"

"Yes. Molly called me to offer me my last payment, then tried to get me to give it back. Why do they need money? Why did she sell her Hummels?"

He shrugged. "Unless you suddenly become her best friend, you'll never know."

She chewed thoughtfully. "I have Lloyd on it." She set down her fork. Lloyd...

Connor snorted. "Yeah, well, if they were stolen, he might be able to help you, but...what. What's that expression on your face?"

She shook her head. "Just thinking."

"About what?"

"Never mind." She set down her fork and stared at her almost empty plate. "I feel much better now. I hate being hungry."

"I'll make a note."

She hopped off the stool. "But now that I'm *not* hungry..." She slid her arms around his neck. "Since you did the inviting in the first place, what, exactly, did you have in mind?"

He put his hands on her waist and pulled her close. He could feel every curve. Her eyes were bright and her lips looked good enough to eat.

"I'm not so good with words. Why don't I show you?"

And he did.

7

The next morning's breakfast went off without a hitch.

The venue was outdoors again, this time on the grounds of a stately mansion that had been chosen as a Mansion in May, a fund-raising project for the local hospital. Every year, a significant—and empty—building was found, designers from all over the state re-did the various rooms, and then people paid twenty-five dollars to walk through. This breakfast was a week before the current Mansion in May project opened to the public, as a thank-you to the designers and other participants, and to let them preview the Mansion. The morning was sunny and breezy, and all the guests seemed to be enjoying themselves despite the long round of speeches.

Jo, leaning against the side of one to the Luxe vans, nudged Enza. "This is what the Junior League looks like?"

Enza squinted. "I'm not sure these are Junior Leaguers or not. They could just be hospital board people. Or hospital board people's wives. Or maybe just well-meaning really rich people?"

Jo sighed. "Must be nice to have so much money."

"Yeah," Enza said with a grin. "But seriously, do these women look happy?"

"Actually, no," Jo said slowly. "In fact, they look way too serious, considering they're eating French toast with candied pecans and maple glazed bacon. Maybe they're all vegans?"

Enza snorted. "No. Those are the ones eating fruit salad and non-dairy muffins. And they don't look happy either. Listen, did you happen to notice Molly and Lloyd last weekend?"

Jo frowned. "Molly and Lloyd?"

"Yeah. Like, did it look like they were, you know, *bonding*?"

"I just noticed Lloyd falling over himself for Phyl."

Enza nodded slowly. "Me too. But before that..."

She straightened and went over to Phyl.

Phyl was standing next to a table loaded with food. Enza looked over Phyl's shoulder. "It appears we didn't run out of food after all."

Gina, manning the French toast station, giggled.

Phyl sighed. "Yes, I think we're going to be fine. But if everyone wants seconds..."

Enza snorted. "If everyone has seconds, they'll have to roll themselves outta here. Listen, before you and Lloyd had your cosmic moment, did he and Molly...talk?"

Phyl shook her head. "I don't know. I think—wait. Yes. He and Molly did have some sort of conversation. They were talking about music. He said she was very interested in something he'd played, some old Irish tune. He said she was quite sentimental about it." She looked at Enza closely. "Why?"

"Someone needs to talk to her," Enza said. "And it can't be me, or any of us. But maybe Lloyd?"

Phyl frowned. "You want him to, what, be a spy for you?"

Enza made a face. "Oh, stop being so dramatic. I just need a bit of information. Do you think he'd be willing to talk to her?"

"And how, exactly, would that happen? He can't just go knock of her door."

Enza nodded. "True. But, can you ask him? Or better yet, is he meeting you today after this? At the office?"

Phyl nodded slowly. "Maybe."

Enza rolled her eyes. "Oh, come on, Phyl. What?"

"I wouldn't feel very comfortable asking him to do something like that as a *personal* favor."

Enza looked at her partner warily. "What are you getting at?"

Phyl lifted her eyebrows, looking completely innocent. "Maybe if he were an employee? Then, I wouldn't feel like I was *imposing* on him. You know?"

Enza tightened her lips. "That's very sneaky, Phyl."

"Probably. He has a gig tonight, playing somewhere in Whippany. He was coming by my apartment first, but I'll have him come to the office instead. And then you can offer him a job?"

Enza folded her arms across her chest. "You are a very surprising woman, Phyl. I feel like you've had all these hidden layers, and they are just now coming to the surface."

Phyl smiled sweetly. "Layers. Yes, I have layers. Should I have him come to Morristown?"

Enza nodded, then strode back to Jo.

Jo saw the look on her face and frowned. "What?"

"It looks like we're hiring Lloyd."

"What? Why on earth would we do that?"

"Because he needs to talk to Molly McGowan for me, and I'm not above paying him to do it."

Jo shook her head. "You're the boss, I guess, but I don't see this ending well."

Enza shrugged. "At least it will make Phyl happy. And we could have used an extra set of hands this morning. He may work out just fine."

Jo patted Enza's arm. "Famous last words."

ENZA EXPLAINED to Lloyd what she needed, and he listened patiently, nodding.

"Well, I have to say that Mrs. McGowan and I did indeed have a few very nice moments there, right before the body was found, that is."

Enza smiled. "I'm sure."

"Mrs. McGowan has quite a colorful past, you see. She had a mad passion for a fiddle player back in the old country but, alas, she had to break his heart."

Enza nodded sympathetically. "I see."

Lloyd sipped his coffee and glanced at Phyl who sat quietly at his side. "So, the plan would be for me to, quite accidentally, of course, bump into her, invite her for a bit of something-something, and then, how can I put this? Pump her for information?"

Enza beamed. "Exactly."

"And how and where, exactly, would this happen?"

"She goes to mass every Sunday at St. Timothy's. Now, there's only one—"

"A church?" Lloyd squawked, his eyes opening wide. "You want me to stalk her in a *church*?"

"Well, you can't knock on the front door and accidentally run into her," Enza said reasonably.

"But..." He put the coffee cup down so abruptly that some liquid spilled over onto the counter. "I haven't been inside a church in a *very* long time."

"And I don't know what mass she attends. I thought we'd park outside at the first mass, and when we see her go in, you could follow..."

"But, but, then I'd have to *sit* through mass."

Enza leaned toward him. "Are you worried about a lightning strike, Lloyd?"

He looked at Phyl, his face pale. "Now, Phyllis, darlin', you know I'd do anything for you, but this..."

Phyl reached over and patted his hand. "And I know you would, love. Which is why I wouldn't just *ask* you." She looked sharply at Enza. "Right?"

Enza cleared her throat. "Right. Phyllis would never impose upon your, ah, friendship with something like this, Lloyd. It wouldn't be right. This is not coming from her at all. It's coming from me. As your, ah, employer."

Lloyd tilted his head, his eyes suddenly bright. "Employer?"

"Yes. It seems that we have the need for an extra hand. Why, this morning we were practically frantic. I realize that your band keeps you quite busy, so it's possible that you don't *need* another job, but—"

He held up his hand. "Say no more. I know that Phyllis and I had discussed this earlier, and she told me how short-handed you were. I would surely hate to leave you ladies in a lurch if I could be of any assistance. As it happens, I could certainly use a bit of extra cash."

"Yes. Well, we couldn't put you on a salary, of course. A simple hourly wage? Say ten dollars an hour?"

"Fifteen," he shot back.

Enza drummed her nails against the countertop. "We

need to count on you during the week. We have two events coming up, one next Tuesday, and then Thursday night."

"Not a problem," Lloyd said.

"You'd have to help set up. It's not glamorous work by any means."

"I'm not afraid of a bit of hard work, dearie. I've done worse for less."

"Yes," Enza muttered. "I'm sure."

Lloyd sniffed. "I accept your offer."

"Excellent. The first mass at St. Timothy's is at eight. I'll meet you there."

He paled, then lifted his chin. "And I'll be on the clock?"

"Yes," Enza said.

Lloyd frowned. "I know St. Timothy's. There's a little coffee shop right down the block. I could accidentally bump into her, as she's *leaving* mass, you understand, and the two of us could sit and chat. I buy her coffee, get her talking, then take her home. Easy-peasy."

"That's a very good idea," Enza said slowly. "Is there any way I would to be able to hear what's being said?"

"Ah. Yes. Of course. That coffee shop? There are double rows of booths, right down the middle. You find a place to sit, and I'll do the rest. I'll meet you in the parking lot by 7:30. Molly strikes me as the type of woman who would never be late to anything as important as mass. And if she doesn't attend the first mass, well, we can just wait. On the clock."

Enza narrowed her eyes. "Yes. On the clock."

"And I won't be mentioning this to my dear nephew tonight. No, not at all."

Enza felt a little jolt in her stomach. "You're seeing Connor tonight?"

"Well, I told you. We have a gig. Would you be stopping

by, perhaps? Just to say hello?" He grinned at her. "I imagine he'd like to see you again."

"He's already seen me again," Enza said coolly. "But tell him I said hi."

Lloyd cackled. "You're going to lead that boy on a merry chase, aren't you?"

"I have no idea what you're talking about," Enza said, standing and smoothing down the front of her dress.

"Yes, you do. And good luck, dearie. He needs a woman like you, I think. Usually, women fall into his arms without so much as a where's-your-father. He needs a challenge."

She felt herself getting red. She hadn't been much of a challenge. She glanced at Phyl, who was looking at Lloyd with a serene expression on her face.

"We're done here," Enza said. "I'll see you Sunday morning.

Lloyd beamed. "I'll even wear my good suit. And tie."

"Perfect," Enza muttered.

MOLLY ARRIVED for mass at 7:53. Lloyd and Enza watched her as she climbed the steps, head down, not greeting any other churchgoers.

"You'd think she'd at least know some of the other church ladies," Lloyd said.

Enza watched. "I don't think Molly is the type to foster many close friendships."

"True that. She was pleasant enough to me and the boys, but there was plenty of tension running around that party," Lloyd said.

Enza looked over. "What do you mean?"

Lloyd shrugged. "There were money problems. Molly, ah, confided a bit with me."

Enza narrowed her eyes. "Did you tell the police this?"

"O' course." Lloyd looked shocked. "I would never be holding back important information now, would I?"

"I don't know, Lloyd. Considering what I can imagine was a rather dicey relationship with the police in the past..."

"There is nothing more respectful than an ex-con," Lloyd said. "I told them everything that Molly told me."

"Which was?"

"That her allowance had been cut. Considerably. That her banker had closed up all but one of her accounts, and her savings were down to nothing."

"They were planning to send her to a nursing home," Enza said. "That just makes sense. Faith was the one with the money, and I'm sure she didn't want Molly to take any of it with her. If something happened while Molly was in the home, it could all be taken away."

Lloyd nodded. "Aye, that's all true."

"Did she tell you about her figurines?"

"Them Hummel things? Indeed. She had to sell them off."

Enza exhaled loudly. Why hadn't she spoken to Lloyd earlier? He seemed to be a fountain of information. "What did she need the money for? I mean, she couldn't have had many expenses."

Lloyd shook his head. "She was rather vague about that. I think that Linda—was that her name—Faith's sister? Anyway, Linda was in some sort of trouble, and Molly was helping her out."

Linda? Enza drummed her nails along the steering wheel. Linda was in trouble with money? And Molly was helping her out? "What kind of trouble?"

Lloyd shook his head. "No idea."

"Then maybe that's where you should start. If Linda was

so desperate that Molly was selling off her beloved Hummels, then maybe she was desperate enough to kill her sister."

Lloyd nodded. "Got it."

They sat in companionable silence, then Enza cleared her throat. "So, what can you tell me about Connor?"

Lloyd raised his eyebrows. "Aside from...what? He's been a Federal agent for a long time, likes to go off camping by himself, and plays a mean guitar."

"He camps?" Enza shuddered. If that's how he liked to spend his leisure time... "Why did Connor get divorced?"

"His job. He was spending a lot of time on the road, you see. That takes a toll. And Laura was a bit of a needy thing, she was. Some women require a bit more attention than others, and Laura was not one to be happy on her own. They were still quite friendly in the end, no drama, but still, he thought she was the one."

"And since then?"

"Well, when she left him, he started playing with the band. I think he needed something to fill the weekends, if you get my understanding. So I have to be honest here, there wasn't a lot of time when my dear nephew was without female company. But his approach is whatcha-call hit-and-run. Until now, that is." He gave Enza the side-eye. "I think he finds you a much different kettle of fish."

Enza smiled smugly. "I am." She glanced at her watch. "I'm going to find a seat in the coffee shop."

"Fine. Make sure you sit in the back, and your back to the door. Put your hair up. She's seen it down, and we don't want her to even *think* you look familiar. Reading a newspaper would be good, it hides more of your face. I'll ring you, just one ring, when she comes out of the church. That's when you place your order because we don't want her hearing your voice. Just look at the menu and drink coffee until then. I'll make sure that her back is to you. It shouldn't be too busy and noisy at this early hour, but I'll try to get her within earshot. If not, I've got as good a memory as anyone."

Enza grinned. "Lloyd, I think that you're a pretty good choice for this assignment."

He sighed. "It's good to put my God-given talent toward something that won't land me in jail." He got out of the car and walked across the street, and Enza drove on.

IT WORKED out exactly as they'd planned. Enza sat, her back to the door, and drank coffee until her phone rang once, then ordered French toast, bacon, and fresh fruit. She was starving, but also counted on eating the fruit last, and as slowly as she needed to.

As for Lloyd, as soon as he saw Molly step down the church steps, he put on his best smile and moved, quickly and quietly, until he was behind her.

"Mrs. McGowan? Molly? Why, as I live and breathe. I've been walking down this block for years, on my way home from my Sunday breakfast, and to think, you've been walking the same path."

Molly's eyes lit up and she put a hand out to touch Lloyd's sleeve. "Oh, Lloyd, how good to see you. You're almost an answer to my prayers."

He tucked her hand in his arm and walked beside her. "And what prayers were those?"

She sighed. "Someone to talk to. There's a weighing on my mind, Lloyd."

"Ah, my dear Molly, do you believe in fate? Is it possible there's a reason I just happened to see you today, of all days, when I've spent years on this same sidewalk? How about a cup of tea? There's a bit of a place around the corner."

She nodded. "That would be lovely, Lloyd. And tea...just the thing, I think. And maybe a muffin?"

Lloyd, with an advance from Enza in his wallet, nodded. "Certainly. Why, you can have a full breakfast if you feel the need. Ah, here we are. Mind the step..."

He spotted Enza, and the booth directly in front of her was empty. The waitress obligingly led them down the aisle, and Molly slid in, her back just inches from Enza.

"We'll be having two menus if you please," Lloyd said. "Coffee for me, and tea for the lady."

The waitress left, and Molly frowned. "Didn't you say you just came from breakfast?"

"Ah, yes, but you see, the pancakes here are supposed to be light as featherbeds. And I'm a man of hearty appetites." He reached over and took her clenched fist in his hands. "Molly, what is it that's troubling you so?"

Enza, concentrating on what was going on behind her and completely ignoring her breakfast, leaned back against the worn leather of the bench.

Molly took a deep breath. "I feel just terrible about Faith," she said in a low voice. "Lord knows, I never cared for the woman. In fact, I fairly despised her, and hated the fact that she had my only son wrapped so tightly around her finger. But to see her dead..."

Enza frowned. This was not what she was expecting to hear.

The waitress delivered coffee and tea and took a brief order—pancakes and a toasted blueberry muffin.

"I can only imagine," Lloyd soothed. "A young and healthy woman like Faith, such a kind and thoughtful person, cut down in her prime. Who, do you think, could have done such a thing?"

Enza held her breath.

"She was not so kind," Molly said. "Don't be believing everything you heard from those party planning women. She had them fooled, Faith did. She had everyone fooled."

Enza broke off a piece of French toast and lifted the fork to her mouth, chewing thoughtfully. It was not nearly as good as Phyl's.

"Oh?" Lloyd asked. "And how was that, exactly?"

"Richard was afraid of her," Molly said, her voice dropping so low that Enza had to strain to hear.

"Afraid? Of his own wife?"

"She had the money," Molly went on. "And she had been asking an awful lot of questions about her accounts."

Lloyd made a clucking kind of noise. "Now, married folks often quarrel about money. At least, that's what I've always heard."

"But...well, her sister..."

Enza leaned back again.

"Yes?" Lloyd said.

"Linda had asked her for money, too."

"Whatever for?" Lloyd asked gently.

Molly sighed. "Linda told me that she had a, well, a bit of a gambling problem. And she owed money to some very unsavory people. I tried to help, even Richard tried, but Faith wouldn't give a cent."

Lloyd clucked again. "Gambling is the devil's own work, Molly. You know that."

"Linda has a sickness. To keep her from paying her debts is the same as holding back medicine. She needed that money, and not even Richard could get it from Faith."

Enza stopped chewing. Why would Richard try to get money for Linda? Surely, he knew how his wife felt her.

The food appeared, and there were a few moments of silence as Molly broke apart her muffin and chewed a tiny fragment.

"The thing is, Lloyd, I'm afraid that Linda may have killed her sister. If Richard had access to the money, all of Linda's problems would be solved." Molly's voice had a bit of a tremor. "I may be living with a murderer, Lloyd. And I may be keeping the truth from the police. What should I do?"

Lloyd, his mouth full of pancake, shook his fork at Molly before swallowing. "Now, Molly, I must say, I'm not ordinarily a fan of the police. My relationship with the law has been strained in the past. But we're talking about your eternal soul, here."

"I know," Molly said in a weak voice. "But I love Linda. She's been the daughter to me that Faith never was. I've already given so much to help her."

Enza had to clench the edge of the table to keep from getting up, turning around, and smacking Molly McGowan upside the head. She thought Linda killed Faith? And she hadn't said a word to the police? What—

Lloyd, however, saved the moment. "Have you any proof, Molly? Anything concrete? After all, police have theories of their own. I'm thinkin' they don't need any more.

Molly shook her head. "Just a feeling. Since poor Faith's death, Linda has been a different person. As though her troubles are almost over."

"So, Richard has agreed to give her what she needs?" Lloyd asked.

Enza could practically hear the wheels turning in Molly's head. "No, he hasn't. At least, not that I've been privy to, and they haven't spent any time alone together to talk about it. And Linda...well, she was desperate there for a while. I gave her money, a lot of money, and that kind of eased the situation, I think, but then things got very bad again. But now...I think she's told whoever she owes money to that it's coming. And soon. I overheard her on the phone."

"Then, Molly, how do you think she's getting the money?" Lloyd asked.

"I don't know," Molly said, her voice stronger. "I don't know why Linda would have said something like that."

"Something like what?"

"Like...she said that in just a few weeks everything would be just as it was always supposed to be."

"Who was she talkin' to? Do you know?"

"No. And I know I wasn't supposed to hear."

"Was Linda expecting money of her own? From Faith?"

Enza silently high fived Lloyd for asking the right questions.

Molly made a snorting kind of noise. "Money from Faith? When pigs fly. I bet she wasn't left a penny."

Molly broke apart more of her muffin and watched Lloyd as he ate his pancakes with obvious enjoyment. "You're a good man to talk to, Lloyd," she said. "I've always had a soft spot in my heart for a musician."

"Ah, well, Molly, we're an odd sort, but we enjoy the beauty in life. That makes us such open and honest souls."

Enza almost snorted coffee through her nose.

"When I was younger," Molly said, a soft and wistful note in her voice, "I fell in love."

"Ah, yes," Lloyd said encouragingly. "You said. A fiddler?"

Molly nodded. "Yes. Ian Campbell. He had the most glorious red hair."

"I've always been partial to blondes meself," Lloyd offered.

Maybe that explained Phyllis, Enza thought. She finished her French toast while Molly took a brief trip down memory lane, Lloyd contributing encouraging grunts as he ate. Enza finished her coffee and began to slowly pick at her fruit. If Molly continued like this, they could all be there past lunchtime.

Lloyd obviously had the same thought. "So, Molly, what do you think you're going to do?"

"I'm not sure," Molly sighed. "I want to talk to Richard about this, but he's so wrapped up in his own grief, I don't want to add to his burdens."

"Molly, if you're living with a murderer, isn't Richard as well?" Lloyd asked.

Molly paused, then said slowly, "Why, that's true."

"And where, exactly, does all that money go if something, heaven forbid, should happen to Richard?"

"To me," she whispered, so low that Enza almost missed it.

The waitress appeared with their check, and Lloyd fumbled for some money. "I'm thinkin'," he said when the waitress left, "that you should be talking to someone about this. That police detective, Mr. Whalen seemed to be a very understanding sort."

"I don't know, Lloyd. What if I'm wrong, and Linda is innocent? I could get her into so much trouble."

"True. But who else could have killed Faith?" Lloyd sighed. "There's a lot at stake here, my dear girl."

Enza slowly chewed on a piece of melon and heard them get up and move away. Her waitress appeared seconds later.

"Done here? Do you want me to wrap that fruit?"

The fruit tasted like wet cardboard. Enza shook her head, dropped a twenty dollar bill on the table, and left.

LLOYD WAS WAITING in front of St. Timothy's and jumped into Enza's car before it came to a complete stop.

What's wrong?" Enza asked as she pulled away from the curb. "You act like you're being chased by someone."

Lloyd shuddered. "It's a church, Enza darlin'. A *church*." He glanced over at her. "Did you get what you wanted?"

Enza shook her head. "Not what I expected."

"And what were you expecting, exactly? For her to break down and confess to murder?"

"I guess not." She stopped the car at a traffic light and tapped her nails impatiently against the steering wheel. "Here's the thing. When we went to pick up our money, she and Linda tried to keep the check for themselves. Why? Did Linda do that because she knew she wasn't getting anything from Richard? Did she need it right away? But for what? It wasn't all *that* much. She's just extremely greedy?"

Lloyd shook his head. "I don't know, but I'm betting that money is at the bottom of all of this. People kill for all sorts of reasons, Enza, but money and love are always at the top of the list."

"I'm sure you know more about that than I do," Enza muttered.

"Aye, you're right there. But here's what I'm thinkin'. When folks are killed for passion—in anger or hatred—it's a spur-of-the-moment thing. But this..."

"Lloyd, she was murdered at a party," Enza said, turning the wheel sharply to pass a sluggish minivan. "That screams spontaneous to me."

"Exactly. At a party, where there would be dozens of

people who would end up being suspects. If she was murdered while alone, sitting quietly at home…"

Enza chewed her lower lip. "I've got to go to the gym and think about this. Where am I dropping you again?"

"Phyl's place."

She glanced over at him. "I don't know if I've mentioned this, but if you hurt her…"

He held up both hands. "Yes. I know. Believe me, I know."

Phyl was renting a townhouse in Cedar Knolls, so Enza dropped Lloyd off before driving to the gym, where she spent the first twenty minutes of her time as she always did —on the treadmill, running as fast as the machine would allow.

She was also thinking hard. Lloyd was right. The party had provided someone with enough distraction to allow them to slip into the kitchen, then into the den, and out again. With so many guests, not to mention the Luxe crew, who would have noticed? Obviously, no one.

It was all rather ingenious.

Whoever killed Faith took one look at the invitation and knew the time had come.

But Linda?

She moved from the treadmill to begin the circuit of machines. She set the weights on autopilot: she'd been working out at the same place for the past three years. She took deep, steady breaths and…pushed.

Linda needed money to pay gambling debts. She'd already gone to Molly, and Richard, and probably her sister…she was nearing the end of her rope. She must have been feeling the pressure, and the party came at the perfect time. But…too perfect?

Enza felt the burn in her thighs and finished her count. She lay there, frowning.

Something wasn't quite right.

Virginia? Faith had called her deranged and hinted that she'd done something in the past. Maybe if she could find out what that was? And that scarf...did Virginia kill Faith, then run into Molly's room to hide, dropping her scarf when she heard the police arrive? When did Virginia *leave* the party?

She moved to the next machine, set the weights and grasped the handles, and took another breath.

But Linda...had she been thinking about killing Faith *before* she knew there was going to be a party?

It would help to know how much Linda owed, and when she had to pay up. Enza knew nothing about gambling beyond a few trips to Atlantic City. How on earth could she get that information?

She stopped. Surely Lloyd...

And it would help if she could dig up the previous incident between Faith and Virginia. Maybe Lloyd again?

She clenched her fists again and pulled hard. She almost cut her session short to drive back to Phyl's but remembered the leftover mini chocolate lava cakes in the walk-in. She set her teeth, finished the circuit, and put in a call to Phyl.

8

Connor sent a text. *Had a gig the other night. Lloyd said you said hi. You could have just as easily stopped by and said it to me personally but...how about dinner tonight?*

Sure. I'll bring Thai

How about we meet at Red Dog Tavern at 7

?????

I'm thinking we could spend time together with our clothes on

Enza grinned. *As in... date?*

Let's go crazy

Already there!

Perfect, she thought. In a public place, she could talk about the murder without worrying about him getting too loud.

When she arrived, he was sitting at the bar. She slid on the stool beside him and waved at the bartender. "Hey, Doug. The usual."

Connor raised his eyebrows. "You're a regular?"

She shrugged. "Not really. But bartenders always seem to remember me."

He sipped his beer slowly. "I bet. The table will be ready in a bit. How was your weekend? Did your breakfast go okay?

She nodded. "Perfect. Everyone seemed very pleased, and the chairperson already told us she wants us again next year."

"Good. Excellent. And yesterday?"

"I met some Brooklyn friends in Manhattan. Dinner. How was your gig?"

"A gig. You know, I show up, play some music, spot a sexy woman, someone gets killed..."

She laughed. "Typical Saturday night."

He nodded. "Yep. I guess today was a day of well-deserved rest?"

She took a quick drink of her wine. A nice Shiraz. Had he spoken to Lloyd? "No. I had a few things to take care of. Non-work-related things."

He looked at her steadily. "Faith McGowan related things?"

"So, Lloyd did talk to you?"

He rolled his eyes. "Enza, I think you need to stop and take a look at what you're doing here. Using an ex-con to stalk a woman in a church?"

"No. Lloyd wouldn't set foot in the church. He grabbed her outside, on the sidewalk. And he got some very useful information. Did he tell you?"

"No, he didn't," Connor said. "Because I made it clear to him I didn't want to know."

"Oh, come on, where's your professional curiosity? Linda had a gambling problem. *Has* a problem. She was desperate for money."

He narrowed his eyes. "Is that another piece of information that Whalen doesn't have?"

She took another sip. "If Whalen is any kind of cop, he knows about it, and he also knows how much she owes and to whom, which is more than I've got. For now, anyway."

He shook his head. "You realize it's kind of against the law to interfere with the investigation of a crime?"

"I'm not interfering. At all. I'm just asking a few questions on my own, just to make sure that justice will be done. I'm big on that, you know. Justice."

"The police are doing their job."

"Then why haven't they made an arrest?" She raised both eyebrows over the rim of her glass.

"There's a process," Connor said. "And the police are carefully looking everywhere."

"They weren't looking at Virginia Crewe, and they should have been. What about Linda's gambling?"

"I'm sure they're aware of something like that."

"So, can you find out how much she owed? And to whom?"

He set down his glass, rather forcefully. "Enza…"

"That way I won't need Lloyd to snoop around for me."

"Enza…"

"Look. This is what I've got. At first, I thought that Molly got rid of her Hummels to get enough money to hire a hitman to have Faith killed."

His brows drew together. "Ah…what?"

"But, obviously, that's wrong because she gave her money to Linda."

"Well," he shrugged. "Obviously."

"Linda owes money. Molly gave it to her, but it wasn't enough. Linda went to her sister, who said no. Then she went to Richard, and maybe Richard asked Faith, Faith said no, so Richard tried to get the money some other way, and

Trulove was helping him move cash around, and Faith found out."

"Seriously?"

"Absolutely. This opens up an entirely new avenue of investigation."

"New avenue? Of investigation?" He echoed faintly.

"Yes." She said, warming up to the whole idea. "Richard and Truelove were manipulating Faith's accounts to cover Linda's debt."

He stared mouth slightly open. "Are you serious?"

She nodded. "That happens to be a perfectly plausible explanation."

"And why, exactly, would Richard go against his wife's wishes and give money to Linda? Surely he knew there were bad feelings between them."

Enza paused. Hmmm... he had a point. "Maybe Molly asked Richard, and Richard didn't know anything about Linda, he thought he was getting the money for his mother?"

"And why would Molly need money? She was living with them and going into a nursing home." He set down his glass and leaned his forearms against the bar. "It seems to me that if I was Trulove, and a client of mine asked me to break several Federal laws that could get me sent to prison, I'd need a very good reason. What reason could Richard have told him?"

She frowned. Another good point. A thought struck her. "Trulove had Linda's picture in his office. Maybe they had a relationship? Maybe...maybe Trulove knew all about Linda and her problems with gambling, and that's why he was willing to fiddle with the books when Richard asked."

"But that doesn't answer the question of why Richard would do something to help Linda in the first place." He shook his head and laughed. "Oh, my God. Enza, how did you come up with such a cockamamie scenario?"

The bartender leaned over and whispered to Connor, who slid off the barstool. "Let's go. The table is ready."

Enza tilted the glass to get the last few drops, shimmied off the stool, and shook down her dress. She beamed at the bartender, who stared openly. "Thanks, Doug. Perfect as always." She turned to Connor and glared. "And that is not a cockamamie scenario. It's perfectly logical."

Connor rolled his eyes. "No, it's not. I swear, the only person at the party who's not a suspect is Richard and me."

"Oh, I've got a theory about Richard, too."

"Why? Because he was probably the only person that Faith would have let in that room in the first place?"

She shook her head. "No. But I keep thinking that the door *wasn't* locked. I mean, maybe I heard it click, but maybe not, and anybody could have slipped in there..."

"How long do you spend thinking about this case? All your working hours?"

She slid her arm through his as they walked to the dining room. "All the working hours I don't spend thinking about what I'd like to do to you," she murmured.

He looked down at her and almost walked into the doorway.

"Careful there," she said, pulling him to safety. "You're no good to me damaged."

He swore quietly under his breath.

"So," she said as she sat down, "you gonna get me the info on Linda's debts or what?"

Connor carefully studied the menu, trying to rein in his frustration and imagination. "I'm not on the case. You do realize that, don't you? And unlike whatever you may see on television, I just can't saunter into Whalen's office and expect him to tell me anything."

"You're friends. I bet you could. And while you're at it, find out about Virginia's scarf."

He glared over the top of the menu. "What scarf?"

"The one I found in Molly's closet. Virginia could have killed Faith, then hidden in Molly's closet, then slipped out the front door."

He lowered his menu. "You found what? In where...how? So now *Virginia* killed Faith? How many of these theories do you *have*?"

"Listen, I'm just exploring all the possibilities. Even the extreme ones. You have to have an open mind about these things."

"Of course," he said faintly.

"Which is why I need your help to find out some basic information so I can narrow down my options." She leaned forward and made a bit of a pouty face. "You are going to help me, aren't you?"

He swore again. "I'm not the sort of man who allows his sex drive to influence all his decisions."

"What decisions *does* your sex drive influence?" Under the table, she slid her foot out of her stiletto and up the inside of his pants leg.

"Well, I may decide to skip dinner altogether," he said, glaring at her again.

"This," she said slowly, "was all your idea." She glanced up at the waiter who had materialized at her shoulder. "I'll have the lobster." She handed over the menu. "Baked potato with extra sour cream and chives. Blue cheese on the salad, and no bread. Please. Oh, and another glass of wine. Doug knows." She smiled sweetly at Connor "You know what they say about lobster?"

His mouth twitched, he swore a third time and then handed over the menu. "The same," he said. "But no wine for me, thanks."

When the waiter left, he leaned forward and dropped his voice. "And just for the record, as much as I do enjoy lobster, it's not just it's, ah, stimulating properties I like, because it's not just your body that interests me. Although," he took in a deep breath, "I have to admit, your body is certainly interesting. The truth is, I mean..." He took in another breath. "Even though your rather obsessive fascination with poor Faith McGowan's murder is infuriating, I think you're about the most intriguing woman I've met in a very long time. And I want to spend more time with you."

The last sentence came out in a long rush. Connor dropped his eyes. In the course of his career, he'd been in the direct line of fire a dozen times. He had talked down a meth head with an AR-15 and interviewed a man who'd eaten his three daughters. But saying those words to Enza felt like the bravest thing he'd ever done.

She reached across the table and squeezed his hand. "Intrigue is my middle name," she cooed. She was about to say something teasing and playful, but the look on his face stopped her. She swallowed and decided that, if ever the time was right, it was now. "And since we're playing true confessions, I have to say your body is starting to take second place to the rest of you. And for me to admit that, well...it's a lot."

There was silence for a very long few seconds.

"So?" Connor said.

"So, I think we have to be careful. Maybe slow things down?"

He nodded and sat back. "That's a good idea. After dinner, I'll just take you home."

Her jaw dropped. "Are you kidding? I don't mean slow *that* down. Oh, honey, absolutely not."

He squeezed his eyes shut and shook his head. "Then what?" he asked He opened his eyes to find her grinning at him.

"We'll figure it out. Starting tomorrow."

His shoulders slumped. "You're going to drive me crazy, aren't you?"

She took her new drink out of the waiter's hand and took a long, slow sip.

"If you're lucky," she said.

IN THE MORNING, despite the rigors of the night before, Enza was dressed early and at her desk and on her second cup of coffee when Jo arrived at nine.

Jo narrowed her eyes at her partner. "What are you doing down here already? Problems with Bridezilla?"

Enza waived her hand, eyes on her computer screen. "Which one? The Basking Ridge princess has some serious competition with this Edgewater widow. I got this email first thing this morning, and it's like, ten pages long. I thought we were going to have a nice, reserved second ceremony for a quiet older couple, and she wants a friggin' live band that covers old disco songs. And a champagne fountain. And she's picked five bridesmaids. Five."

Jo settled into a chair. "Ka-ching."

Enza nodded. "I know. But I can't be chasing down bands right now. I need to know how much money Linda owed, and to who."

Jo frowned, confused. "Linda? I thought the woman's name was Caroline."

"What? Yes, it is. I was talking about Linda Hollowach.

Faith's sister." She swiveled in her chair to look at Jo. "Although Connor seems to think my theories are without much credibility."

Jo raised her eyebrows. "You saw Connor again? Last night? That's, what, three times this week?" She leaned forward. "Enza—"

Enza held up her hand, palm out. "I know. Yes, that does make three times. And for the record, the sex was, once again, amazing. But it's not just that. He's..."

Jo's jaw dropped open as she watched Enza having a hard time as she tried to say what was on her mind. "Enza, do you *like* this guy?"

Enza swallowed. "Maybe. Yes. I mean...yes."

"You've only known him a week," Jo said cautiously.

"I know that, too. So, we agreed to slow things down."

"Was that before or after you took your clothes off?"

Enza sniffed. "Before. But we also agreed that the slow-down would start *today*."

Jo shook her head. "Enza, I have to say, I'm stunned."

Enza folded her hands together. "Me too."

"I've known you for a long time."

"Five years."

"And I've seen you with, well, a lot of men."

"I like men."

"But..."

Enza threw up her hands. "I *know*! I need to step back and look at the big picture." She drummed her nails against the desktop. "Speaking of the big picture, Molly had a collection of valuable antique Hummels that she carefully collected over the years, and she suddenly starts selling them off after she moves in with Richard and Faith. Two weeks before the party, she withdraws a big hunk of money. In the meantime, Faith is rearranging her bank accounts, including taking away the one in Molly's name. This is all about the money, Jo. I know it is."

Jo sat, folded her hands and sighed. "Since you're not letting this go, the best thing to do is try to figure it all out so we can get back to the business that we get *paid* to do. So. It's about money."

Enza nodded. "Yes."

"Faith had it, and Linda needed it, and Faith refused to give it to her."

"Yes."

"Molly gave Linda money?"

"Yes."

"And obviously, Faith found out because she shut Molly down."

Enza frowned. "She shut Molly down...before...I wonder when this gambling problem of Linda's surfaced. Because Molly was cut off a year ago, when she moved in with them."

"Maybe it was just a coincidence?" Jo said. "After all, it just made sense if Molly didn't have any more living expenses."

Enza continued to drum her fingernails. "Molly said that Richard tried to help. Did she mean that Richard gave Linda money too? And maybe that was why Faith rearranged her accounts?"

"Listen, I get there can be bad blood between sisters, but Faith was going through a lot of trouble to keep Linda from paying off her debts."

"Here's the thing," Enza said, leaning forward on the desk. "Connor said something about how Faith would have only opened that locked door for one person."

"Well, that's not Linda," Jo said.

"That's probably true."

"And she wouldn't have opened it for Molly either."

Enza nodded. "Also probably true. So that leaves Richard."

"Richard...what?"

"She only would have opened that door for Richard." Enza looked at Jo across her desk. "She only would have opened the door for *Richard*," she said again, very slowly.

"But..." Jo moved to the edge of her chair. "But Richard... he loved Faith."

"He also loved his mother. And what did Trulove say about it? That he was in agony about sending her away, and it was all Faith's idea?"

"So rather than send his mother to what was probably a very nice nursing home, where he could still see her whenever he wanted, he murdered his wife?

"Hmmm. There had to be more."

Jo sat back. "But then...how about Virginia?

Enza exhaled loudly. "That's right. We need to talk to Virginia."

"That's not what I meant."

"But that's what I need to do. And I also need to ask her how her scarf got into Molly's closet."

"I bet Molly knows," Jo murmured.

"Maybe," Enza said, "but she'll never tell."

"Never tell what?" asked Phyl, coming into the office in a breathless whirl. "You're talking about Molly McGowan, aren't you? She called Lloyd."

Enza sat up, eyes wide. "Molly called Lloyd?"

Phyl sank into a chair and nodded several times. "Yes. I just got off the phone with him myself. They're meeting again. But you have to hurry. She's on her way there now."

"Where?" Enza demanded.

"The house in Montclair. I'd drive you myself, but..."

Enza grabbed her purse and shot from the chair. "I understand, Phyl. Thanks, but I've got this."

THERE WAS STILL yellow crime scene tape across the front and back doors. Enza walked quietly up the drive, listening for any sound of voices. If she still couldn't get in the house, where exactly would Molly ask Lloyd to meet her?

She rounded the corner of the house, peeked into the backyard and saw them.

Linda was sitting on the patio, her face turned away from Enza, watching Molly and Lloyd who were sitting together farther down on the lawn. Enza glanced around. There was no way she could get any closer to hear what they were saying. Not that it mattered. She was certain Lloyd would give her the whole story of what Molly told him. She narrowed her eyes at Linda, then stepped out, mind racing.

Linda turned quickly in her chair, then stood abruptly. "What the hell are you doing here?" she asked.

Enza slowed and tried to look innocent. "What? Me? What are *you* doing here? I'm looking for one of Phyl's serving trays. We can't find it anywhere, and I thought..." She glanced at Molly and Lloyd, still deep in conversation. "Oh. Look at them. I wonder what *that's* about."

Linda looked tired and tightly wound, her skin pale and hair pulled tightly off her face. "Get out of here," she hissed. "You're trespassing."

"Is it your place to tell me to go?" Enza asked, walking closer. "After all, this isn't your house, is it? It's not even Molly's. Technically speaking, you're trespassing too."

Linda glanced toward Molly, then back at Enza, her eyes narrowed.

"Why are you doing this?" she hissed. "Why are you—?"

"I know about the gambling," Enza said, taking a leap. "I know all about it."

Linda tilted her head. "What are you talking about?"

"You and your gambling debts." Enza lifted her chin. "Isn't that why Molly gave you all her money?"

"Right. Gambling." An odd expression crossed Linda's face. "Did she tell you that? When? God, she's such a blind and stupid old woman."

Enza struggled to keep the shock from registering on her face. "I thought that you and Molly were like mother and daughter."

Linda snorted. "Molly would like to think so."

"But she gave you all that money, Linda. Who was it for? Was it ..." she remembered what Helen had said over Rueben sandwiches and Irish coffee. "Was it Richard? Were you in love with him?"

"What? Me and that piece of crap Richard? Are you kidding? Why would I want Faith's sloppy seconds?"

Enza took a mental step back. "Richard didn't seem to be a piece of crap. He seemed..."

"I know how he seemed," Linda spat. "Perfect Richard. He had Faith fooled, he had his mother fooled...he was an idiot. A vain, pompous idiot. I've always felt sorry for Molly. She was so blind when it came to him." She stopped herself and shook her head. "We're all so stupid when it comes to the men in our lives."

"Who were you stupid for?" Enza asked.

Linda's eyes narrowed. "You need to leave," she said in a cold, low voice.

"What about Faith? Was she stupid about Richard?"

Linda took a step toward Enza. "Don't snoop around here anymore. Snooping is what got Faith into trouble in the first place."

Enza narrowed her eyes. "Are you threatening me? What do you know, Linda?"

"Hey!" Molly screeched from across the lawn. "What are you doing here?"

Linda stepped back. "Go," she hissed.

Enza stood as Molly came at her, cane thumping against the patio stone. Lloyd walked behind her, looking shocked.

"Molly, listen—" Enza began

"Get away from us," Molly screamed, cane waving. "You've done enough. Go away."

"Molly, you need to talk to Linda—"

Molly swung the cane at Enza, who jumped back.

Lloyd grabbed Molly's arm. "Now, Molly, —"

Molly whirled around, staring at Lloyd, then slowly turned back to Enza. "You're with her, aren't you," Molly growled. "All this time, it was she who put you up to this."

"Ah, Molly," Lloyd soothed, but Molly was having none of it. She tried to hit him with her cane too, and he ducked and ran around to Enza.

"We need to go," he muttered, pulling at Enza's arm.

Enza needed no further encouragement. She took Lloyd's arm and the two of them hurried toward the driveway.

"Meet me back at the office," Enza called, hopping into her car.

Lloyd waved, and she drove off.

"CALM DOWN," Jo said again. "Deep breaths."

Enza was pacing up and down the small hallway between the lounge and the kitchen. "Where the hell is he?"

Phyl was right behind her, nervous fingers tugging at the end of her long braid. "Lloyd is very cautious behind the wheel," Phyl said. "More than me, even. He'll be here any second."

"There's something wrong. Molly thought that Linda had a gambling problem, but when I asked Linda...I think Linda just made that up to get the money. But why else would she need it?" Enza said, half to herself. "And what was the deal with Richard?"

"What are you talking about?" Jo asked.

"Linda said Richard was a pompous idiot, that he'd fooled Molly, and he'd fooled Faith."

Phyl looked shocked. "But I thought that Richard was, well, perfect."

"No one is perfect," Enza muttered. "Connor said something like that about Faith, remember? We have no idea what Richard is really like."

Lloyd came in, whistling tunelessly and carrying a brown paper bag. Enza stared at him.

"You stopped for groceries?" she asked, incredulous.

"I felt the need for a bit o' something. My, that woman has a temper."

"You mean Molly?" Enza yelled, following him into the kitchen.

He pulled out a long, slender bottle and took a glass from the dish drainer. "O' course, Molly. She called me, you know. Said she was going to the police but wanted to talk to me first. Like a rehearsal, she said. She was going to turn Linda over to the police, tell them about her gambling, everything." He unscrewed the cap and poured until the glass was half full. Enza grabbed the glass from the counter, downed the contents in one gulp, and set the glass down again with a definite thump.

Lloyd sighed, poured again, and drank it himself.

"Things were almost going fine until you showed up. My, she can turn on a dime, that one." He poured a bit more.

Which Enza promptly drank. "What did she tell you?"

"That she found paperwork. Linda owed money on her townhouse. Her bank accounts were empty. All the money that Molly had given her was gone, but Linda said she needed more. Molly made her promise, you see. That if Molly gave her the money, she'd stop with the gambling. But Linda didn't stop, so Molly was going to turn her in."

"I'm guessing Linda wasn't gambling," Enza muttered, watching Lloyd pour.

"To be honest, I haven't been able to find a whisper about Linda and any debts. And I know the people who would be the definitive authority on such a matter," Lloyd said, taking a small sip.

Enza took the glass and took another, much longer sip. It didn't have that bite Jameson had. Lloyd had excellent taste in Irish whiskey. "Linda needed the money for something else. We have to find out what. And we also have to find out more about Richard."

"Maybe we could find out about Linda's money situation through Trulove," Jo said.

Enza waggled her finger. "Right. Trulove. You said he had a picture of Linda?"

Jo nodded. "Yes. One of those dreamy glamour shots, all smoky eye and soft focus."

"I didn't see them together at all during the party," Phyl said.

Lloyd, taking back his glass and refilling it, sniffed. "Why would someone invite a banker to a birthday party anyway?"

"Good question," Enza muttered. "Did Molly spend much time talking to him?" she asked Jo.

Jo shrugged. "I wasn't paying all that much attention, but

I don't think anybody spent much time talking to him. He just kinda sat there and drank tea."

"And he was one of the last to leave," Enza said. "Give me a bit more of that, Lloyd. I think it's loosening up my memory."

He frowned. "Watch the way you're knockin' back that whiskey, young lady, or it'll loosen up a lot more than your memory." He handed back the glass. "You're dealing with my mother's milk there."

Enza narrowed her eyes and at him as she smiled. She took another very long swallow of whiskey and set it down with a flourish. "What if Linda and Trulove were in it together?"

Lloyd's eyes popped. "You mean they were makin' the beast with two backs?"

Enza stared, then burst into giggles. "The beast with what?"

Lloyd carried the glass to the sink. "You know exactly what I'm talkin' about now. And him a respectable banker."

"We don't know he's respectable. At all. Maybe he's a first-class crook."

Lloyd made a small face. "I can check into that if you'd like."

"Enza," Jo said in a quiet, patient voice. "I think you're getting a little carried away. Earlier today, in this very same office, you were convinced that Richard killed Faith."

"It all makes sense," Enza said. She held up one finger. "Linda lied to get Molly to give her money." She held up another. "Linda gave all the money to someone else, cause Molly said her bank accounts were empty." She held up a third finger. "Linda called Richard a piece of crap, thereby putting into very serious question the whole *isn't Richard a great guy* theory." She held up a fourth finger. "She also said that women got stupid for the men in their lives." She stuck out her thumb. "Maybe the man in her life was Trulove. Richard said Trulove was in deep. Trulove said he was on board." She waved her hand toward Jo. "What does that spell?"

Jo sighed. "It spells Enza finally found a drink she can't handle."

"No. It spells Linda knows who killed Faith. And maybe it was Trulove. We need to look at all those bank accounts and see what was going on. It's always about the money." Enza looked around, saw a chair, and very deliberately sat down in it. "My tongue feels funny."

Lloyd made a clucking sound. "This isn't like that wine you drink, Enza darlin'. This here packs a bit more of a kick."

"What you need to do is call the police in the morning," Jo said. "I'm sure those nice detectives will be more than happy to hear all about this."

Enza squinted hard at Lloyd. "When was Molly going to the police?"

Lloyd took the bottle from the table, checked the level through the brown of the glass and made a small clucking noise. "Well, before you showed up and spoiled everything, she was going to go first thing tomorrow morning. But who knows what's going to happen now."

Enza dropped her voice to a low whisper. "Do you think Linda will kill Molly? She wants to spend the rest of her life in a nice house. Not in the big house."

Lloyd shook his head. "The way Molly spoke of her, like the daughter she never had, I don't think so."

"But here's the thing. Linda didn't feel the same way about Molly. She was putting on an act. But why?"

"There are all sorts of reasons for her to lie. Still," Lloyd said. "Molly'd be a whole lot harder to kill."

Enza nodded and waggled her finger. "True dat." She looked around for the glass, and, unable to find it, fixed her eye on the bottle and crooked her finger. "Slide that big boy over here."

Lloyd grabbed the bottle and held it high over his head. "I don't think so."

Jo shook her head and tugged at Enza's arm. "Why don't we put you upstairs, a little closer to bed?"

Enza drew back, indignant. "Bed? It's still light outside."

"Yes," Jo said, trying not to grin. "But I don't think that's going to matter much. In fact, in a few minutes, I think you'll be very grateful."

Enza allowed herself to be taken up, where she fell, face first, down on the bed.

"I'm taking your shoes off," Jo told her.

"Doesn't matter," Enza mumbled. "Can't feel my feet."

And that was all.

"Hey."

The voice seemed to come from very far away.

"Enza? You okay?"

She tried to open one eye. Where was that voice? *Who* was that voice?

"Hmmpt."

Laughter. "Oh, Enza, never drink with an Irishman."

She opened one eye cautiously. Connor's face swam into her field of vision. "Am I dead?"

He shook his head, grinning. "No. Why?" He leaned closer and whispered, "Do I look like heaven to you?"

She groaned and turned over, trying to bury her pounding head deeper into the pillow.

"Should I bring up some coffee?" he asked his voice shaking with laughter.

She nodded once, found it too painful, and groaned again.

Her tongue felt like there was something growing on it. Her eyes were heavy. She cautiously wiggled her fingers and toes and breathed a sigh of relief. Last thing she remembered she couldn't feel them at all.

She sat up slowly and opened her eyes. Thankfully, the blinds were still down. She felt, very strongly, that too much sunlight right now would be unbearable.

She smelled the coffee before she saw him, coming through the door with a tray carefully balanced in both hands. He was dressed in a dark navy suit, beautifully cut, a blinding white shirt and a somber gray tie.

"Did you dress to deliver my eulogy?" She asked as he set the tray down on the bed.

He shook his head. "I'm due in court this afternoon. I'm taking the train, then heading into Brooklyn. I just wanted to stop by and see if you were okay. Uncle Lloyd told quite a story about last night."

She drank the coffee gratefully. "I will never drink that poison again."

Connor eased himself onto the other side of the bed and looked at her. "It seems that my Uncle has found an additional source of income, something we should talk about, but not now. Anyway, with extra change in his pocket, he indulges in one of the few legal vices he can enjoy. That poison was ninety-dollar Irish whiskey. Sippin' whiskey, we call it. And for good reason."

She shuddered and drank more coffee.

"I got a phone call this morning from Whalen. About Virginia Crewe."

Enza's head turned so quickly it hurt. "Did they question her about that scarf? I bet she broke down and confessed. You should have heard her fighting with Faith—"

"She's dead," Connor said quietly. "Found early this morning in her apartment. Stabbed through the heart with a knife from her own kitchen."

She slowly put the coffee cup back down on the tray. "Oh. But...God, that's awful. So...a second victim?"

"That's Whalen's thinking. He's focusing on Linda and Trulove." He shifted on the bed a bit. "Lloyd told me about yesterday. What did Linda say to you?"

"Linda lied to Molly and told her she had a gambling problem. Molly sold all her Hummels to help Linda pay off her "debt". But she needed more money, and Molly started to balk." Enza frowned, trying to remember. "Linda said Richard was a piece of crap who had fooled everyone, including Faith." She sat up a bit straighter. "Listen, I think that the two of them have some sort of relationship beyond both knowing Molly. Trulove had a picture of Linda in his office, but at the party, he acted like he didn't even know her. And why was he there anyway? Who invites their banker to a party? I mean, if he was just paying a respectful social call, why was he still there after almost everyone else had left?"

"Many criminals remain at the scene of the crime just to watch how it all plays out. Sometimes it's ego. They want affirmation for being so clever. Sometimes it's just curiosity."

She stared into her half-empty cup. "Then Trulove killed Faith? But why?"

"If Richard lost Faith's money, and was trying to cover it up, Trulove would be the one to do it. They're following the paper trail now."

"Linda needed the money so that Trulove could replace what was missing out of Faith's accounts?"

Connor shrugged. "Maybe."

"Faith found out?"

"Maybe."

"And started asking questions. Linda said that snooping is what got Faith in trouble in the first place."

"Well, she's very right there. Snooping into business that isn't yours can get you into trouble."

She met his eyes. "So far, snooping has gotten me a great man and a brutal hangover. I'll take it."

He leaned over and kissed her. "So maybe now is the time to call it quits."

"As long as Whalen stays on track."

"Tell you what. If you promise to back off, I'll call him again and let you know what's going on."

"Thanks." She put the empty coffee cup on the tray and pushed it away. "I feel bad for Molly. Linda...I don't know why Linda was pretending to be such a good friend to Molly. She called her a blind, stupid old woman. And Molly thinks of her as the daughter she never had."

"My enemy's enemy is my friend," he said. "Sun-Tzu, *The Art of War*." He signed. "Besides, women like Molly tend to create their own realities, Enza. It's never pleasant when they're shown to be false, but I can't feel sorry for people like that. Remember, she hated a perfectly decent woman, Faith, and for what reason? I bet she couldn't even tell you why."

He got off the bed and slid his hands into his pants pockets and looked around her bedroom. "This is quite a place you've got here, I have to say," he said, taking in the deep green wallpaper, thickly hung drapes, and polished hardwood floor. He took a few steps forward and peeked into her closet. "All those clothes are yours?"

She cautiously stretched, then nodded. "Yes. I like wearing clothes." He glanced at her and she gave him a quick wink. "Sometimes."

He held both hands in front of him, as to ward off a blow. "Stop. I mean it. I have to catch a train."

She waved a hand. "You're safe. I think it's going to take another hour or so before I can stand up."

He grinned. "I believe it. I'll call you tonight."

She watched him walk out the door, then sank back into bed.

Trulove and Linda. It made perfect sense.

Then she pulled herself up and out of bed. As much as she would have liked to sleep the rest of her headache away, she felt a niggling worry about Molly.

Lloyd was right. She'd be much harder to kill than Faith. But she was in Linda's house, with Richard away at work...

She needed to make sure that Molly went back to the police.

Today.

9

W hen Enza finally made it downstairs, she heard a low rumble of conversation, and then some high-pitched laughter. She peeked into the lounge.

Phyl and Jo were both there, with three well-dressed women, ranging in age from early twenties to AARP.

"Hi," she said brightly. "I didn't know we had any appointments today."

Jo waved a hand. "My fault. This is Emily Rapinowsi, Shelia Fields and Monica St. Simon. They're all members of the Tri-Delta sorority, of which I am a proud alumna, and they want us to throw their Mid-Atlantic reunion."

Enza, who had graduated from Brooklyn College and had always viewed sororities as only for the rich and connected, felt suddenly out of place. She had always laughingly called her education "The School of Hard Knocks." Having worked her way through in six years combining night classes with whatever part-time work she could find, these women, with their sleek outfits and perfect make-up, were the only type of women she felt less than confident around.

"I never knew you were a sorority girl, Jo," she said.

Phyl raised her hand. "Me too. Delta Zeta. UConn class of '86."

The youngest of the woman, Sheila Fields, leaned toward Phyl. "We won't hold it against you."

Monica St. Simon, in what was unquestionably a Chanel suit and hair that matched the creamy white of her pearls, smiled sweetly. "We have a big reunion for the New York and New Jersey area women alumna every five years, and of course we try to find one of our sisters to help with the event. Luckily, Joanna here is not only a distinguished alum, but she is also part of one of the most talked-about party panning outfits around. A win-win for us."

Enza went into her best We-can-make-it-happen mode. "Well, we always do our best for our clients, but I can imagine that Jo will make sure there's a little bit extra going into your reunion. When is it?"

"We always try for the spring. April 13th of next year. It's a Saturday night, and since we had our last reunion in New York, we're looking for a venue here in Jersey," Emily Rapinowsi explained. Enza put Emily's age anywhere between thirty and fifty-five, depending on whether to factor in plastic surgery or not.

"Well, that certainly gives us enough time," Enza said, but really, it didn't. The best venues were usually booked years in advance.

Jo flipped through her Moleskin notebook. "I think I have all the information we need. Emily here lives right in Summit, so she'll be our main contact."

The women all stood and shook hands, and Jo walked

them out. Enza sank into a chair and glanced at Phyl, who rolled her eyes.

"April?" Phyl said. "They think we can find someplace for April?"

"How many people?" Enza asked.

"Two hundred," Phyl answered.

Enza shook her head. "Never gonna happen."

Jo came in and slumped into the chair across from Enza. "How are we ever going to find a place for two hundred people on a weekend in the spring?"

"Why didn't you just tell them that right away?" Enza asked.

"Because they're Tri-Delt, that's why," Jo answered miserably. "And so am I."

"You're also a professional who knows better," Enza pointed out.

Jo shook her head. "I'll start making calls now. Do we have anything going on April 13th that we could possibly cancel or reschedule?"

Enza glared. "You did not just say that."

Jo muttered under her breath. "No, I didn't."

She got up and hurried to her office.

Enza closed her eyes. The headache was gone, and her tongue and various other body parts were all back to normal. But there was something in the back of her brain that she wasn't quite comfortable with.

"Are you okay?" Phyl asked gently. "Lloyd was rather worried about you last night."

"I'm fine. Although I will never drink anything with that man again. Or any other Irishman who walks in with a bottle in a brown paper bag. I'm sticking to red wine, with the occasional champagne." She opened her eyes. "I need to see Molly. Virginia Crewe was murdered last night."

Phyl's jaw dropped. "No."

"Yes. They're looking hard at Miles Trulove and Linda Hollowach, and Molly is right there, in Linda's house."

Phyl shook her head. "But surely Linda wouldn't hurt Molly? They're like mother and daughter."

Molly might be harder to kill than Faith had been, Enza thought, but that didn't mean it couldn't be done.

ENZA RANG the bell at Linda Hollowach's townhouse a second time. She peered through the narrow sidelight window. Yes, there it was again. A flicker of movement, but no one had come to answer the door.

"Molly?" she called, hitting the door with her open palm. "I know you're in there. Please open the door."

She was about to give up when the door was abruptly opened. By Richard.

"Ah. Oh. Richard. I was hoping to speak to your mother."

He looked older, his face pale and his usually smooth dark hair slightly mussed. He was dressed in rather loose-fitting jeans and a faded red T-shirt. "So I hear. Whatever could you want to speak to my mother *about?*"

"I just heard about poor Virginia, and I know that she and Molly were close..."

"They were not close," Richard said. "That is, my mother is a kind woman who didn't want to hurt Virginia's feelings by shutting her out. Any closeness was purely on Ginny's part."

Enza took a moment to let that sink in. "I see." She glanced around Richard to see Molly standing, slumped against her cane, at the back of the hallway. She looked up at Richard. "Has she been back to see Detective Whalen?"

Richards's dark eyes narrowed. "Why would she do that?" he asked.

Enza heard the thump of Molly's cane as she came forward. "Let her in, Richard. She's just concerned."

Richard took a long beat before stepping back, and as Enza crossed the threshold and heard the door close behind her, she felt a chill up her back.

"Tea?" Molly offered. Without hearing her reply, she turned and thumped her way to the kitchen. Enza followed, aware that Richard was behind her.

Enza sat as Molly filled the kettle. "Poor Ginny." Molly shook her head as she set the kettle on the stove. "Never had a bit of luck, that girl."

Enza cleared her throat. "Where's Linda?"

Molly made an elaborate showing of spooning the tea into a white china teapot. "Linda? I believe she's at work. Did she go to work, Richard?"

Richard, leaning against the doorjamb, nodded. "Yes. She went to work."

Molly sat down heavily across from Enza. "We're all just trying to get our lives back to normal," she said.

Enza nodded. "Of course. Molly, do you know how Virginia's scarf ended in your room?"

Molly tilted her head. "And how would you be knowing about that?" she asked softly.

"I'm the one who found it," Enza told her.

"Ah." Molly nodded, as though to herself. "Well, Ginny probably went to use the bathroom, right there off the kitchen, and it was occupied, so she went and used the one in my room. And, well, the scarf just fell off." She smiled brightly. "See?"

"I found it in the closet, Molly. Not in the bathroom."

Molly nodded again. "Ah, yes. You see that's where *I*

found it. In the bathroom. And I knew it was hers and put it in my closet to give to her the next time I saw her."

"So, you just threw it on the floor?"

Molly glanced at Richard. "Of course not. I hung it on a hanger and it must have just slipped off."

"Right."

The kettle began to whistle, and Enza watched as Molly stood, pulled the kettle from the heat and carefully poured the water into the teapot. She brought the teapot to the table, then the teacups and saucers, one at a time, and finally, the sugar bowl. Richard did not move to help her, but stood there, in silence.

Enza murmured thanks as Molly filled her teacup. "And when, exactly, did you do all that, Molly?" she asked, spooning sugar.

"Oh. I don't recollect, exactly." Molly waved her spoon around. "Does it really matter?"

Enza sipped. "You see, I saw Virginia wearing the scarf after five. I found her in the den, arguing with Faith, and she was wearing it then. You were outside. Remember? You asked Richard to keep the music going. And I don't remember you coming up to the house. At all. Until after Faith..." Enza glanced at Richard, whose face was still and watchful. "Until after the police had arrived."

Molly stirred her tea, the spoon making a faint click as it hit the sides of the cup.

Richard cleared his throat. "As soon as she learned about...what happened, she went straight to her room. Didn't you, Mother?"

Molly nodded.

"She needed time alone to compose herself," Richard went on. "That's probably when she found poor Ginny's scarf."

Enza sipped more tea. "So, it's not like you found it somewhere else? Like, in the kitchen?" Like, Enza thought, where Virginia dropped it when she saw the murderer coming out of the den and probably ran for her own life.

Molly's lips formed a thin line. "No. Not in the kitchen."

Enza could hear the faint dripping of water from the faucet in the silence. "Why haven't you talked to Detective Whalen?" she asked. "Yesterday you were all ready to go over and tell him your concerns."

"Linda had nothing to do with this horrible business," Molly said shortly. "I was just workin' myself up about nothin' at all."

"Did you at least talk to Linda—?"

"I think you're upsetting my mother," Richard said, his voice steady but Enza could feel the threat in the room.

"Well, I just wanted to see how you were," she said at last. "I'll see myself out."

She rose and walked back to the front door, aware of Richard behind her. She opened the door.

"Don't come back here," he said quietly, and the front door shut tight.

PHYL WAS in the downstairs kitchen. They had a luncheon for fifty the next day, and Phyl was carefully icing chocolate cupcakes with caramel icing. Lloyd was sitting on a stool along the long stainless steel worktable that ran down the center of the room, whistling tunelessly.

Phyl sighed quietly with pure happiness. Here she was, doing what she loved, in the company of a most extraordinary man, and life simply could not get any better.

Lloyd looked up as Enza came down the stairs. "This woman, she's a marvel," he crooned.

"I know," Enza said. "Anything I can eat that won't send my blood sugar through the roof?"

Phyl nodded toward the walk-in fridge. "Deviled eggs, potato salad, and individual peach tarts. But don't eat too much. I don't..."

"I know. You don't want to run out of food tomorrow." Enza went into the walk-in, then came out with a single tart and a few deviled eggs on a simple white plate. She perched on a stool next to Lloyd.

"Did Connor tell you?" she asked him. "Virginia Crewe was murdered last night."

Lloyd let out a low whistle. "Now, I wonder what that poor woman knew?"

Phyl felt a pang of sorrow. That sad, frightened woman. She leaned against the stainless steel counter. "What happened?"

"She was stabbed. With a kitchen knife."

Phyl shuddered. "Any idea why?"

Enza shrugged and took a nibble of peach tart. "I'd say Lloyd here just hit the nail on the head. She knew something. Or saw something." Enza's brow furrowed, a sign, Phyl knew, that she was thinking fast. "She saw someone come out of that den and knew something was wrong. Maybe whoever it was hadn't seen *her*, so she backed away and hid in Molly's closet, hoping to wait it out until the end of the party." She took another bite. "Trulove. I bet she saw Trulove come out, knew that he had no business being there, and took off."

Phyl stuck her knife back into the bowl of frosting. "But Mr. Trulove would have no reason to kill Faith."

"Oh no," Enza shook her head. "He had plenty of reason. He and Richard were stealing from Faith. Who knows, maybe for years."

"Then why couldn't Richard be the killer?" Phyl asked, smoothing the top of a cupcake.

Enza paused, stared at the half-eaten tart, and frowned.

Lloyd made a clucking noise. "She has a point, there, Enza darlin'."

Phyl pointed her knife. "You've been saying all along it's about the money, and who had the most to gain?"

Enza's phone made a chirping noise. She took it out and looked at the screen. "It's Connor," she said slowly. "Trulove has been arrested."

Lloyd clapped his hands together. "You were right, Enza. I have to take my hat off to you. A fine bit of work right there, figuring all that out."

Enza shook her head. "Lloyd, there's something really strange about this whole thing." She quickly told them both about the conversation she'd just had with Molly and Richard.

Phyl, cupcake in one hand and spatula in the other, made a face. "Well, you are right. That certainly sounds odd."

"Partic'ly since she was so determined on Sunday to go to the police," Lloyd said. "And even up until yesterday, before you broke in like a bull in a china shop."

Enza finished her tart and brushed the crumbs off her fingertips. "I did not break in anywhere. I was right there, outside on the patio." She stopped. "Talking to Linda," she finished.

Phyl saw Enza's face change. "What?" Phyl asked, lowly lowering the spatula.

"Linda said something about how stupid we were about the men in our lives. She wasn't talking about Richard, so it had to be Trulove. She knew all along he'd done it. She must have told Molly, and *that's* why Molly never went to the police."

"Makes sense, I suppose," Phyl said. She wrinkled her nose at Lloyd. "I can certainly understand the getting stupid part."

Lloyd began to blush, and Enza slid off the stool. "I'm upstairs if you need me," she said, and hurried away.

Phyl and Lloyd looked at each other.

"Is that me you're talkin' about?" Lloyd asked. "Do you think you're doing something stupid?"

Phyl leaned over to kiss him on the lips. "I can understand it. Of course I can. But whatever is happening between you and me? I have a feeling it's probably the smartest thing I've ever done."

Lloyd grinned. "I'm feelin' the same, Phyl darlin'. Feelin' the same."

JO CAME in a few minutes later to find Enza sitting in the lounge, her high-heels off, rubbing the ball of her foot and looking very serious.

"What?" Jo asked.

"Virginia Crewe was murdered last night. Trulove has been arrested."

"Oh—wow."

"Yes. Wow. Just when I was beginning to think that maybe Trulove didn't do it after all..."

"Listen," Jo said. "I found a place."

Enza blinked. "A place? For what?"

"The Tri-Deltas, of course. Do you know that brick monstrosity on Old Mendham Road that's been vacant forever? It's going to be the next Mansion in May, the hospital fundraiser. I was just meeting with next year's organizers, and mentioned how it would make a terrific venue, and how we happened to be *looking* for a venue, and...guess what?"

Enza cocked her head. "One of those organizers is a Tri-Delt?"

Jo grinned. "Yep. Talk about luck! So, they're going to let us use the ballroom for the Tri-Delta reunion. Its only two weeks before the official opening. Oh, and we're set for the breakfast again next year too."

Enza grinned back at her partner. "Jo, I've got to hand it to you. Quick thinking. Congrats."

Jo made a huge show of trying to appear modest. "Yes, well, you know. All part of the Luxe experience: great food, one-of-a-kind venues, pulling a rabbit out of a hat..."

Enza laughed. "Yep. That's us."

Jo tilted her head. "And it looks like your mystery is also solved, so you can get back to concentrating on, you know, the luncheon tomorrow, and the weekend coming up—a birthday and a retirement and that wine tasting."

Enza nodded. "Yes. Mystery solved. Trulove was the bad guy after all—a crook and a killer and he was probably stringing Linda along, so we can add a broken heart to his list of crimes."

Jo made a face. "I hope they lock him up and throw away the key."

Enza sat, absently rubbing her foot, trying to figure out why she wasn't happy about Trulove being arrested. "If only Richard and Molly hadn't been so weird," she said softly. "Why were they so..."

Her phone chirped again. And it was Richard.

Sorry I was so abrupt today. I'd like to explain and apologize. Can you meet me at the house in Montclair?

She stared at the phone. She couldn't care less about an apology, but an explanation...

Be there in half hour she texted back.

Thank you

She looked at her high heels. "That was Richard," she said.

"What?" Jo frowned. What's going on?"

She slid her feet back into the heels. "He wants to apologize. And explain."

"Are you okay with going over there?" Jo asked.

"Listen. If he has any explanations, I want to hear them."

Jo shrugged. "Whatever. I'm going to tell Emily the good news," she said, and practically danced out of the room.

And just when her feet were starting to feel almost normal. "This better be good, Richie-boy," she muttered, "Cause my feet are killing me."

IT WAS GETTING dark as she pulled up the drive to Richard's house. There were no lights on, and the crime scene tape was still up. Surely he'd been told by the police he could return home. But then, why was the tape still across all the doorways?

She walked around to the back, and there he was, sitting in a chair, dressed very differently than he'd been earlier in the day: dark suit, pale blue shirt, and gray tie. His shoes were polished loafers, and he was drinking from a large balloon brandy glass.

"Ah, Ms. Biondi," he said, standing as he saw her. "Can I get you a bit of something?" His voice was hearty and had a bit of a lilt to it. The old, charming Richard was back.

She shook her head. "No, thanks. I'm still recovering from the bit of something I had last night."

She sat next to him in the faux-wicker lounge chair. "Are you allowed back in the house? I imagine now that Trulove has been arrested, the case is closed."

Richard took a deep breath and shook his head regretfully. "Sadly, no. The case is not closed. My dear friend Miles Trulove has indeed been arrested, on bank fraud charges. Possibly out-and-out theft. But not murder. Not yet, anyway." He took a long sip of brandy. "And I'm not sure they'll ever get it out of him. He's a tough bird, Miles."

Enza didn't let the expression on her face change, even as she felt the beginning of fear send her blood pounding. "Oh?"

He nodded, stretched out his legs in front of him, and tightened his lips. "You see, I don't think Miles is the type of man to be bullied into a false confession. They may think he did it. I'm sure they think they've got the right man. She went to see my mother, Ginny did. Told her all about seeing the killer come out of the den, and how she'd been scared out of her wits. She'd run and hid in Mother's room."

Enza swallowed. "Really? That's what I thought. That Ginny had seen something, and that's what got her killed."

"Yes. But you see Ginny didn't see Miles come out of the den. She saw me." He drained the glass. "I didn't see *her*, of course. I was really in something of a state. After all, I'd just stabbed my wife to death."

He leaned across the arm of the chair, his handsome face inches from Enza's. "Mother doesn't know, of course. And I'd rather she never finds out."

Enza's brain raced. They were so close that there was no way she could get away from him. No matter how fast she moved he only had to stretch out his arm to grab hers. And once he had her, she didn't think she would have the strength to get away. She cleared her throat.

"Where does Linda fit into all this?" she asked, desperate to keep him talking until she could figure a way out.

Richard put his empty glass on a low side table. "Oh, they'd been going at it for years, those two. Linda, well, I think she loved him. Miles just loved money. It was useful, though. When I was trying to talk Miles into helping me with my problems, he talked to Linda about it. She just hated Faith." Richard shook his head and sighed. "She kind of encouraged him to go along. In fact, she helped get some of the money I needed to cover my losses."

"*You* were gambling?" Enza asked.

He uttered a sharp bark of a laugh. "The stock market is just as addictive as the craps table. It wasn't too bad a first, you know. A few thousand here and there. But..."

He looked out across the yard, now growing dark. "I wasn't ready to give any of this up."

"You killed Faith for the money?"

He turned suddenly, his face contorted in anger. "What? Is that what you think? Faith had more money than even I could lose, and she would have given me as much as I wanted if I'd asked her. I mean, I didn't want her to know what a fool I'd been. Of course not. That's why Miles and I tried so hard to cover up my...mistakes." He sat back again. "No. It wasn't money."

Enza leaned forward, genuinely curious now despite her fear. "Then why, Richard?"

He lifted his shoulders, then let them drop. "She was going to send Mother away."

The night noises were coming up, and Enza could hear crickets and the occasional whine of a passing car. "What?"

Richard shook his head. "I could never let Mother go to one of those places. It would have killed her. And after everything she'd done for me..." He exhaled loudly. "I tried to talk to Faith. I even warned her that this could break our marriage, but she had dug in. What else could I have done?"

Enza stared down at the concrete patio. She eased her feet out of her heels and nudged them to the side. If she was going to have any chance of getting away, she'd have to get off fast and run like the devil. She drew her arm off the edge of the chair, as far away from Richard as she could. Now, a distraction.

"When Trulove doesn't confess, Richard, the police will come after you."

"Well, maybe. Maybe not. Linda is a pretty good suspect, don't you think? And Miles may very well throw her right under the bus."

"Your mom is a pretty good suspect as well, you know."

He shook his head. "No. She was out here, right by the band, the whole time. I made sure Miles kept her away from the house."

"Wait...Miles knew what you were going to do?" She remembered what Richard had said...that Trulove should just do his job. And his job had been to keep Molly away from the murder. "And you think he won't tell the police everything to cut a deal?" She was on the edge of the seat now, and she had the balls of her feet square beneath her. She would be able to throw herself away from Robert and take off at a run. He looked fit enough, but she hadn't spent years on the treadmill running full out for nothing.

At least she hoped not.

But she needed him off-balance.

"It was your mother's money," she said.

He frowned. "What?"

"All those Hummel figurines she'd collected over the years. Linda lied to her, and Molly sold them, gave the money to Linda, who gave it to Trulove..."

His frowned deepened. "Linda...lied to my mother?"

"She thought your mother was a fool," Enza said, her words coming faster. "She told me that, right here, on this patio. That she only pretended to like Molly. Called her a blind and stupid fool."

His face turned suddenly ugly, lips twisted, eyes narrowed and his teeth gleaming against his skin. She saw it then, the madness, and she bolted from the chair.

His arm shot out and closed on the cloth of her skirt, jerking her back, and she went down onto the concrete. She felt the impact in her knees and brought up an arm to shield her face as she fell forward. She tried to twist away, but he was right on top of her legs, and she felt him crawling his way up her body.

Adrenaline kicked in, and she heaved herself to one side, shifting his weight, and as she grabbed at the leg of the chair to find something— anything —to hold on to, her hand closed on the pointy toe of her shoe. She held it tightly and swung back as hard as she could.

The heel caught him squarely on his cheek, and he grunted in pain. She swung again and he screamed as she felt the heel go deep into soft tissue. He rolled off her and she was up and off, running toward the driveway, screaming as loudly as she could.

As she rounded the corner, she realized her purse was somewhere back on the patio, with her car keys. The thought didn't stop her for a second. She ran past her car, fighting to control her breath. If she had to run barefoot to the center of Montclair to the police station, she would.

The headlights of a car flashed in her eyes as she pounded down the driveway and she swerved, feeling the grass against the soles of her feet. She was just at the street when she realized that someone was calling her name. She slowed and turned.

Connor was there, running up to her, still in his dark suit and looking like a dream come true.

He grabbed both her arms. "Are you hurt?"

She shook her head.

"What happened?"

"Richard killed Faith," she gasped.

He looked over his shoulder back at the house. Enza faintly heard a hoarse, sobbing sound.

"What did you do?"

"I hit him with my shoe."

He stared, swore, and let go of her as he turned toward the house. She fell forward against him, and one arm went around her as he reached for his cell phone with the other.

"Your shoe?"

She nodded and felt her arms go around him and she stood there, she didn't know for how long, until he'd stopped talking on the phone and his head was against hers. His voice was soft in her ear when she heard the sirens.

JO'S FACE was flushed with anger and her foot was tapping against the tile floor. "I can't believe," she said between clenched teeth, "that I am here again, with you, in a police station, and you with only one shoe." She glared at Enza's feet. "Where's the other shoe?"

Enza curled the toes of her bare foot. "I think the police are keeping it for a while. I used it to stab Richard McGowan in the eye."

Jo's foot stopped tapping and she turned pale. She stopped being angry enough to see Enza clearly for the first time: the skinned knees, the tangled hair, and the bruise on her cheek. "What?"

"It was all I had," Enza explained wearily. "And I had to do something."

Jo sat down next to Enza on the narrow bench. "Did Richard kill Faith?" she whispered in disbelief.

Enza nodded. "And Virginia Crewe."

"Where is he now?"

"In surgery."

Jo ran her fingers through her red hair, loosening the bun. "He killed two women, and yet you still felt compelled to go and talk to him? Alone?"

Enza slipped her other foot out of her high heel. "Trulove had been arrested. I thought they had the killer. And Richard said he wanted to apologize and explain."

Jo tilted her head back against the wall behind her. "Well. Of course." She reached over to grab Enza's hand and squeezed tightly. "Oh, honey, he could have killed you too."

Enza squeezed back. "Yeah."

They were silent for a few minutes. Jo exhaled loudly. "Enza, it's one in the morning and we have a sit-down luncheon for sixty people in less than twelve hours. We're never going to make it."

Enza shook their still-entangled hands. "That's why I called you and not Phyl. We can be as spaced out as we want, but the food has to be spot on."

Jo glared, then glanced up as Connor Ives and Detective Whalen rounded the corner, their heads close, talking. Rather, Whalen was talking, and Connor was nodding his head, his face grim.

"Last time you tried to play Nancy Drew, they almost locked you up for breaking and entering," Jo reminded Enza in a low voice. "I see attempted murder in your future."

"He grabbed me," Enza hissed. "And I was in genuine fear for my life cause, you know, he just told me he'd knocked off two other women. I think justifiable needs to be in there somewhere."

Connor and Whalen stopped in the middle of the hallway, Whalen's arms waving, Connor still nodding his head. Finally, Whalen stopped, looked over at Enza, and straightened his shoulders.

"Here he comes," Jo said under her breath, pulling her hand from Enza's and sitting up straight.

Whalen stood over Enza and Jo, hands on his hips. "Ms. Biondi," he said. His voice cracked a bit, and he cleared his throat. "Ms. Biondi, Richard McGowan is out of surgery and, although he will probably lose his eye, he'll survive."

Enza lifted her chin. "It's better than he deserves," she said.

Jo slumped down a bit lower on the bench. As much as she admired—and at times envied—her partner's gumption, other times she wished Enza would just smile and nod, like a good little girl.

But then, she doubted that Enza had ever been a good little girl.

Whalen cleared his throat. "We found an eight-inch butcher knife hidden behind a cushion on one of the chairs on the patio. We're assuming he lured you to the house to kill you."

"Ya think?" Enza said.

Jo poked her with her elbow. Hard.

"Miles Trulove, upon hearing that McGowan was in custody, has changed his statement. Seems like he knew of McGowan's plan to murder Faith and acted as a lookout. His job was to keep anyone who happened by away from the den. Unfortunately, Virginia Crewe was standing outside of the French doors when Richard came out of the den after stabbing his wife. Trulove saw her slip away and told McGowan."

"I have a question," Enza said.

Whalen rolled his eyes. "Really?"

"Did you talk to Linda? Why did they try to keep that check from me? I mean, it wasn't all that much, and with Faith dead, she didn't need to give any more money to Trulove, did she?"

Whalen pursed his lips. "Good question. And we have an answer. Ms. Hollowach was trying to get away. She was planning on leaving the country and was a little short on the airfare. That's not what she told Molly McGowan, of course."

"She spent an awful lot of her time lying to Molly," Enza said.

Whalen tightened his lips. "Speaking of which, Molly McGowan wants us to charge you with aggravated assault."

Enza bolted upright. "Oh, she does, does she? Where is that wicked old witch? I'll—"

Whalen held up a hand. "The District Attorney did not seem receptive to the idea, especially after we discovered the knife and the large heavy-duty plastic bags that McGowan had stashed in a bench on the patio."

Jo turned to Enza. "See? You are such an idiot."

"I thought Trulove had done it!" Enza said, her voice creeping into a whine from exhaustion, frustration, and the residual fear. "If I had known—"

"Enza," Connor said quietly. "It's over. For now, anyway. I've convinced the very nice detective here to let you go home."

Jo stood up. "Let's go. I'll get my car and meet you out front."

Connor put up a hand. "I've got this," he said. "She probably shouldn't be alone tonight anyway."

Jo looked down at Enza. "You good with that?"

Enza nodded, and Jo sniffed and shouldered her way past Connor and Whalen.

THE CORRIDOR WAS QUIET. Enza tore her gaze from Connor and stared at the floor. She'd seen that the even tone in his voice was in complete contradiction to his eyes, which were snapping with emotion. Was it anger? She didn't want him to be mad at her. More than anything else in the world at that moment, she didn't want him to be mad at her.

Whalen pointed a finger. "You could have been killed."

She looked up and nodded.

"You're lucky Connor here showed up when he did."

Enza arched an eyebrow, and Connor's eyes suddenly changed. "Actually, when I showed up, she was already out in front of the house." His mouth twitched as he looked at her. "Where were you going?"

"To the police station," she said.

"But you were running," Connor said.

"Yeah, well, I wasn't going to go back to the patio and look for my car keys."

His mouth twitched again. "You were barefoot."

"It's hard to run in heels. Especially if only one of them is functional."

Whalen dropped his head and shook it. He gave Connor a long look. "Good luck, my friend," he said, then walked away.

Connor held out his hand and, when she took it, he pulled her up and close enough that she could feel the heat of his body through his white shirt.

"You scared the hell out of me," he said roughly. "If you hadn't told Jo where you were going…"

"Is that how you knew where I was?" She could see the dark hairs of his chest peeking out from where he'd loosened his tie and unbuttoned the top button of his shirt.

"I was on my way back from court and thought I'd drop by, just to…check out all that closet space in your bedroom."

"Yeah," she said. "I've got a lot of closet space." She leaned against him and his arms went around her. They stood for a long time, not speaking, standing in the middle of the hallway in their own little world as people walked around them.

"So," she said at last, "take me home?"

He kissed her softly. "Please, don't ever do that to me again."

She smiled crookedly. "I never make a promise I don't think I can keep."

"So, what…you'll just periodically drive me completely crazy?"

She smiled again, a very different smile. "Oh, no. I plan on doing that on a regular basis."

His jaw dropped open, then he threw back his head and laughed. "I'll take it."

"You bet you will," she said, and they walked out of the station together.

The End